Westside Tigers

Westside Tigers
Age of Innocence

Terry Stroot

PALMETTO

P U B L I S H I N G

Charleston, SC

www.PalmettoPublishing.com

Paperback ISBN: 9798822959811

Table of Contents

Introduction

The Westside Tigers Age of Innocence covers multi genera-tions, immigration, race, and abject poverty. *Tigers* centers on a small-town neighborhood (Westside) and those families that settled there. The book follows the Roemers' leaving Germany, the Lindquists' leaving Sweden, and the Peerys' leaving St. Joseph, Missouri and how they settled on the Westside of Wabasha, Minnesota. The second definition of *tiger* is fierce, determined, ambitious, strong and courageous. The reader will find all those qualities in the Westside families. Those fami-lies survived abject poverty, the Great Depression, and World War II. Not only to survive but flourish and prosper. They had another quality, and that quality was acceptance. The accep-tance of people down on their luck. I leave to the reader to figure out why the Westside was a special and magical neigh-borhood. I am sure there were a thousand neighborhoods like the Westside in America at that time. For those Boomers that grew up in the '50s or '60s, reading *Westside Tigers* will be a trip down memory lane. For those Millennials that that grew up in the '80s and '90s, you will finally understand your par-ents. For those labeled as Generation Z, you reading *Tigers* was like me taking Greek in college: you won't get it.

by Terry Stroot

CHAPTER 1

Okna, Sweden

The village of Okna, Sweden, was a small farming village 155 miles east of Gotenborg and one hundred miles West of Stockholm. In 1830 Sweden was ninety percent farmers. Not large farms, but small plots that could support a family. Farms consisted of a small barn, a chicken coop, and a silo. Animals consisted of a dozen pigs, several cows, and dozens of chickens. Work on the farm lasted most of the day. Chores included slopping the hogs, feeding the cows and chickens, gathering the eggs, and tending the garden. This was where Gustava Lindquist was born in 1831. Her parents were Jonas and Maria Johnson Lindquist.

Okna had birthing rituals, passed on from generation to generation. It centered on the midwife, who was highly respected and possessed extensive knowledge of birthing practices. The whole village would be involved in the birth. The villagers would gather clean linens, warm blankets, and herbs for postpartum care. The midwife would check on the expectant mother several times a week. Family members and close friends would often be present to offer encouragement and assistance. Every new baby was a joy for the village. The village would support the mother, ensuring a safe delivery. After the birth, the village would celebrate the arrival of a new life. This reflected the close-knit nature of the community and the importance placed on the well-being of both the mother and child.After Gustava's birth, the village celebrated for weeks. Family and friends would visit the house, bringing gifts and well wishes. The baby would be given a name chosen from family tradition or religious customs. The naming ceremony was an important event, symbolizing the child's integration into the village. Gustava was named after the Gustaf III, the King of Sweden, who ruled from 1772 to 1792. Gustaf III was nicknamed King Charming, because he praised the farmers and reined in the nobles. Gustava was the second born of her family. Her older brother, Peter, was born in 1829. Gustava was followed by Kristina, born in 1834, Carl August, born in 1837, Axel Peter, in 1840, and Frans Peter, in 1843.

When Gustava was seven years old, she started school. In Sweden at the time, the kids would go to four years of school, called Folkskolan. It was about a mile walk to the one-room schoolhouse from the Lindquist farm. She loved going to school, because she met many girls her age. She loved talking to her new friends. But after four years, she was finished with school. Now the drudgery of farm life began. There were always chores to do. Her parents expected as much from her as her brothers. The family would wake up at dawn, have a hearty breakfast, and start the chores. Her father would assign the chores to the kids. Gustava was always assigned the chore of gathering the eggs. Originally when she started gathering the eggs, the chickens would peck at her hand. The top of her hand looked like a pincushion. Then her father showed her a trick to gathering eggs. Gustava would take the head of the chicken with her one hand and grab the egg with her other hand. When Gustava was seventeen, she could go to the store in town with her parents for the weekly shopping trips. Her dad would hitch the horse to the wagon, and the three of them would go into town. On one of those trips to town, she met Anders Johnson. He was twenty years old and working in his parents' store. When he first saw her, he smiled. Anders had an engaging smile, and he began flirting with her. She was almost swooning. It was the first boy she had met outside of the farm. She fell instantly for him.

Gustava felt like time was standing still till the next shopping trip. On Saturday, Gustava leapt out of bed and was early for breakfast. Her brothers giggled. Gustava's parents dropped her off at the store with the shopping list and continued to the feed store. She loved the time alone with Anders without her parents.

A few weeks later, Gustava's parents said they couldn't go to the store. They had to butcher a hog that day. Gustava said she'd go by herself. She could handle the horse and wagon. Her parents reluctantly agreed. Gustava was bursting at the seams. Her dad hitched the horse to the wagon, her mom gave her the shopping list, and Gustava went to town. When she arrived at the store, Anders was not there. His parents were working instead. Anders parents saw the disappointment in Gustava's face. Gustava did the shopping and was ready to go home, when Anders burst into the store.

Anders walked with her to the wagon and loaded the bags in the wagon. They went for a walk. Anders pulled Gustava into an alley and kissed her. Gustava felt like she was melting. They walked back to the wagon. Anders kissed her again. She swooned. Anders helped her up to wagon.

Gustava started home. From then on, Gustava went alone on the weekly shopping trip. She spent longer and longer on her shopping trips. Her mom asked Gustava if she could ask Anders out for supper some night in the next week. On her next trip to town, Gustava asked Anders to supper Wednesday. Anders heartily agreed.

Anders rode up on his horse to the Lindquist farm. He ran to Gustava and gave her a big hug. They went for a walk holding hands, and she showed him the farm buildings and animals. They bumped into her brothers doing the chores. Gustava introduced Anders to the boys. As the boys continued their chores, they all giggled, especially Frans, who was just turning five years old. Gustava's mom rang the bell on the front porch, signaling that supper was ready. The boys sprinted to the house. The Lindquists ate more or less the same thing every night. A pork chop or a piece of chicken, a vegetable, and mashed potatoes. No salad, no dessert. Water or milk was the beverage. The boys gulped their food down and raced outdoors.

After supper, Anders and Gustava helped clean up the table and washed the dishes. Then Anders and Gustava, with her parents (Jonas and Maria), went to the porch. They chatted for a bit, and then Anders asked Jonas to show him the farm. Gustava was perplexed, because she had just showed Anders the farm when he arrived. When Jonas and Anders returned, Anders said he had to go home. Gustava walked Anders to his horse; they kissed and said goodbye.

The next Saturday Gustava went to town alone with her shopping list. Her heart was racing; she could hardly wait to see Anders. She burst into the store, and Anders was waiting for her. They went for a walk, and Anders was nervous.

She never expected what happened next. Anders asked her to marry him. She was stammering. She was only seventeen. She told Anders that she needed her parents' permission.

"Jonas gave permission last Wednesday when Anders and Jonas were touring the farm," Anders said.

Gustava was speechless. She had so many questions. When would they get married? Where would they live? And how would they support themselves? Anders assured her it was all taken care of. They would live in the apartment above the store. They both would work in the store. Anders's parents were getting older and wanted to take some time off. Gustava loved the store customers and hated her life on the farm. She was not a farmer. She detested gathering eggs. Anders said, "What is your answer?"

Gustava said yes and she kissed Anders. They would pick the wedding date later. She loved Anders, the store, and Anders's parents. The sun was going down, and she had to get back to the farm. She didn't want to leave Anders. But she was a sensible girl and had to go home. They embraced for a long time. She was crying tears of joy, a joy she never felt before. She was truly in love. Anderes and Gustava picked a wedding date for November 22, 1849, two days after she turned eighteen. The wedding would be at the Lindquist farm. Gustava's maid of honor would be her sister, Kristina. Frans would be the ring bearer. Frans was only six, but he would joyfully walk the ring down the aisle.

The day of the wedding, the sunrise was stunning. That day the skies were bright blue. Gustsava's dad butchered a hog, and it was a grand feast. After the last guest left, Gustava said goodbye to her family. Frans gave her the biggest hug and was crying. Anders hitched the horse to the wagon and helped Gustava up into the wagon. Off they went to town and a new life. Frans ran along the wagon with tears in his eyes. Gustava waved goodbye to Frans till her arm was sore. The farm disappeared into the setting sun.

She was starting a new and exciting life. They went to the apartment above the store. She had never been there before. It was lovely and spacious. In the farmhouse, she had shared a bedroom with her sister, and the five boys shared the other bedroom.

The next day, they got up together, had breakfast, and went downstairs to work. They worked seven days a week. Gustava worked the counter, and Anders stocked the shelves. After two months of this routine, Gustava was exhausted. The store work was relentless. At least on the farm, they took Sundays off. She begged Anders for a day off. Gustava was used to hard work, but this was insane. Working twelve hours a day, seven days a week, made farm life look easy. Anders's parents gave Anders a few krona once in a while for spending money. Gustava complained about this also. Anders ignored her. He replied they had an apartment and all the food they wanted. They could help themselves to anything they wanted from the store shelves. Gustava relented, but still pressed for a day off.

Anders asked his parents. Sunday was a slow day, and Anders's parents agreed they could close the store on Sunday. Now Gustava looked forward to Sundays. Anders and she could visit his parents or the farm. Or just rest. The first Sunday off, they visited the Lindquist farm. The day was heavenly. They had a picnic in the backyard and laughed like the old days. The day flew by, and as the sun was setting, it was time to say goodbye. She hugged all of her family members. She cried when she hugged Frans. Frans was nine years old and growing up so fast. Once again life was in balance for Gustava. Then her life was complete when she got pregnant. The next Saturday, when her parents came to shop, they brought Frans along. Gustava told her parents the happy news. The following Saturday her parents brought blankets and gifts for the expectant mother. Gustava's baby would be their first grandchild. Gustava gave birth on May 11, 1853. She named the girl Katerina.

Gustava set up a crib in the store behind the counter. The customers would want to hold the baby. The days flew by for Gustava. Sundays were heavenly. If Anders and she did not visit the Lindquist farm, they would spend the day at Anders's parents' house. Once in a while, they would lie around the store, rest, and catch up on chores. Katerina was now three years old and walking around the store. The store was her playground.

Gustava caught Anders flirting with young girls in the store. The young girls would giggle like Gustava had done when she first met Anders. Gustava thought it was harmless. When Katerina turned five, they had a party in the store. Gustava's parents came into town, and Anders's parents came also. They had a cake and five candles. Some customers brought their little girls for the party. It was a grand party. Gustava tried to get pregnant again, but she had no luck. Then her luck changed. She was pregnant for the second time. She gave birth to a boy on September 4, 1860. She named the boy Peter Johan.

Frans came to the store for the Lindquist shopping trip every Saturday. Gustava really was fond of her younger brother. But Frans was restless. Their older brother, Peter, would be inheriting the farm. Frans hated farm life as much as Gustava. With Peter running the farm now, Frans was just a farm hand. Peter was crabby and always chastised Frans about the way he was doing the chores. Then Frans discovered several articles by Gustaf Unonius. Gustaf had settled in Wisconsin and wrote articles about the excitement of being a pioneer in America. Gustaf had immigrated to Wisconsin in 1841 with his wife. He had settled in Waukesha County, Wisconsin, and founded a settlement he named New Uppsala. He wrote about pioneer life, clearing the wilderness in one of the most beautiful valleys in the world. Swedish newspapers published the Gustaf Unonius articles. After Frans finished reading the articles to Gustava, he noticed she had no reaction. Frans then blurted out that he was going to America. There was nothing for Frans in Sweden. His older brother would get the farm, and besides, he hated farm work.

Gustava finally spoke and said, "You can't go to America and leave me."

Frans abruptly turned around and left the store and went home. Next Saturday Frans told his dad he couldn't go to town and do the shopping trip. He couldn't see Gustava's sad face.

In 1862 Gustaf Unonius published the book *A Pioneer in Northwest America*. It was an instant success in Sweden. Frans got a copy of the book and devoured it. Frans and Gustava mended their relationship, and Frans was excited to see Gustava on his Saturday shopping trips to town. He had just turned nineteen, and the only excitement in his life was his trips into town on Saturday. Gustava's children were nine and two. On Saturdays, when Frans came into the store, they went for a walk. Katerina could mind the store and take care of Peter Johan. On the walk, Gustava told Frans she thought her husband was flirting too much with the girls and ignoring her. Frans talked about how he had no future. He lived in the barn, and his older brother, Peter, lived in the farmhouse with his family. Frans wanted to go to America. His friends were all leaving for America. Gustava protested.

A few years later, in 1867, Gustava was thirty-six, her daughter, Katerina, was fourteen, and her son, Peter Johan, was seven. Katerina was working the store; Peter Johan would help as he could. Gustava was thinking that Anders was more than flirting. He would disappear from the store with a young girl for an hour or two. Gustava confronted him. Anders slapped her. Gustava kept quiet from then on. The usual spring rains of 1867 did not happen. Summer came, and it never rained. The crops dried up. Everybody in the store talked about the drought. Gustava noticed the business in the store was down a bit. Customers were tightening their belts and not buying as much. Frans still came on his weekly shopping trips. Frans and Gustava would visit most of the day. Katerina could take care of the store with Peter Johan's help. They were good kids and worked hard. Frans said the Lindquist farm was going through hard times. The drought was hurting everybody. Frans's older brother Peter was mean and surly to everyone, especially Frans. Gustava complained about her husband and his infidelity. After they talked for a couple of hours, they both felt better. They needed to vent. It was good for both of their souls.

Next Saturday, when Frans came for his shopping trip, they talked about America. Frans read passages from Gustaf

Unonius's book extolling the pioneer life in America. Frans also had a guidebook on how to get to America. The Great Northern Railroad was hiring Swedes in St. Paul, Minnesota, to build tracks to Seattle from St. Paul. The American companies liked the Swedish immigrants, because they were educated and worked hard.

Gustava countered with the Swedish newspapers' view: immigrants to America were lacking in patriotism and moral fiber. No workers were more lazy, immoral, and indifferent than those that immigrated to America. Immigration was denounced as an unreasoning mania or craze, implanted in an ignorant population by outside agents.

To counter Gustava, Frans had an article from the Goteborg Handels newspaper that sarcastically said, "Yes, immigration is indeed a mania. The mania of wanting to eat one's fill after one has worked oneself hungry. The craze of wanting to support oneself and one's family in an honest manner."

Gustava loved the Saturdays with Frans. They could talk about anything, from Anders's infidelity to immigrating to America. Gustava started to sense that Frans would go to America. She would be devastated. Frans was not only her brother, but her best friend.

The winter of 1867/68 was grim for all of Sweden. The summer crop failures of 1867 were widespread. Farmers saved for emergencies like this. They had lots of canned goods in the cellar. The farmers could survive one season of crop failures. They prayed for rains in the spring of 1868. The rains never came. Another crop failure happened in 1868 throughout Sweden. Following the crop failures were mass epidemics. The elderly and infants were especially hard-hit.

Cholera, scarlet fever, yellow fever, and TB were prevalent. From 1867 to 1869, two hundred thousand Swedes died from starvation. Gustava's father-in-law died from cholera in 1868. Gustava's husband left her after the funeral. She never heard from Anders again.

On a Saturday, Frans made his usual trip to town for shopping. The shopping list was short, because the Lindquist farm was doing poorly. Gustava and Frans took a walk. Gustava could see Frans was nervous. Gustava was impatient. She said, "Spit it out, Frans."

Frans finally broke the news; he was going to America in a week. He could no longer be around his older brother. The crop failures were getting to Peter. He was mean, not only to Frans, but to his wife. Peter had started slapping his wife for no apparent reason. Gustava started crying. Her only friend in Okna was Frans. Gustava asked Frans about his trip to America. Frans produced a pamphlet, with instructions on how he would get to America. He would take the stagecoach to Goteborg, take a ship from Goteborg to Hull, England, take a train to Liverpool, and a ship from Liverpool to New York. Then a train from New York to Chicago, change trains to St. Paul, and get off at Minneiska. Gustava worried how Frans would get all that way by himself. He showed Gustava the pamphlet. The pamphlet had lots of detail, plus English words to help Frans make his connections. Finally Gustava asked, "Why Minneiska?"

His friend Lars Olson had immigrated to Minneiska last year, and he wrote glowing letters about Minnesota and Minneiska. Minneiska was on the Mississippi River in a beautiful valley, with a new railroad being built. It was the frontier, and it was booming. Minnesota had just become a state ten years earlier in 1858. Gustava wept. The famine, her husband disappearing, the store failing, and now Frans leaving to America. She would never see him again. Frans leaving was the last painful straw. Instead of crying, she wept uncontrollably. Frans hugged her. They hugged for a long time. He would be back to the store one more time next Saturday before he left to America.

It was a long week for Gustava. Not many customers came to the store during the week. Her daughter, Katerina, was fifteen, and boys were starting to notice her. At times, there were more boys visiting Katerina than customers. The next Saturday, Frans came to the store. Gustava and Frans could feel the tension between them. Frans said "hi" to Katerina, who was giggling with two boys. She didn't answer. Frans went for a walk with Gustava, as there were no customers in the store. They walked in silence for a long time.

Finally Frans blurted out to Gustava that she could come to America with him. Gustava was shocked; she could never leave her home. It was out of the question. She had children to care for. Frans retorted that the children could come along. There was nothing left in Sweden for anybody. Gustava needed a new life and a new start. Gustava was young, only thirty-seven. The children would be fine, and the children could come back to Sweden if they didn't like America. It would be exciting. Gustava got angry at Frans and walked back to the store alone. Frans waited for a time and then followed her back to the store. Gustava was with a customer. Frans went outside and sat on the bench. In a while Gustava came out and sat with Frans. They didn't talk.

Gustava finally said, "I will miss you more than you will ever know. I can't bear seeing you leaving for good."

Frans said, "I will write you monthly letters. You have to think about coming to America later."

They hugged for a long time. The sun was setting, and Frans had to get back to the farm. On his ride to the farm, he thought about his choice. He would miss her deeply, but he had to go. There was nothing in Sweden for him.

Wednesday, Frans rode the stagecoach to Goteborg. He was twenty-five. His eyes were tearing up. He had a lot of doubts. He would never see Gustava, Okna, Sweden, or his friends again. He was really leaving Sweden and going to America. It was not a dream; this was real. During the famine in Sweden, sixty thousand Swedes left Sweden to America in just three years. Eventually 1.3 million Swedes moved to America. Then he started visiting with the other passengers in the coach. The passengers were all going to Minnesota. The excitement filled the coach. His new friends in the coach were all going to St. Paul. Frans had travel companions for the entire journey. It took two months of travel to reach Minnesota.

The train Depot is Minneiska, Mn Train Depot

Frans got off the train in Minneiska. His friend Lars Olson from Okna met him at the train station. There were two riverboats tied up below the train depot. Frans was in awe of the bustling town. Minneiska had been founded in 1854, only fourteen years before Frans's arrival. Minneiska meant "water white" in the Sioux language. Lars became a good friend of Frans. Lars got him a job at the hardware store, and they roomed together in the apartment above the store. New immigrants arrived daily by steamboat or train. The Germans dominated the town, but the Swedes were a close second.

Frans applied for citizenship and changed his name to Frank. The energy of the village was contagious. Frank could feel the energy. Nothing like Okna. He joined the Lutheran church. The church was in the pastor's house; Minneiska didn't really have a Lutheran church. Frank volunteered for the committee to build a proper church. He loved the Lutheran church. The congregation had all come from Sweden in the last ten years. They had similar stories. Frank excitedly wrote his first letter to Gustava. He told Gustava about the town, the Mississippi River, the Lutheran church, and the energy of the town. His excitement grew during the writing of the letter. He ended the letter with how he missed Gustava, but definitely not Sweden.

At twenty-five Frank was full of energy, and he was full of the excitement of pioneer life in America. Working twelve-hour days with Sundays off was nothing for Frank. He had time to go to the saloons and Sunday church. He spent a lot of time during the week planning the new Lutheran church. The church committee drew up plans, raised money, and sought volunteers with building skills. They would start building the church in the spring of 1871. They hired a local contractor, and with the volunteers from the church, the church was completed by October 1871. Frank was proud of his Swedish community. He settled into a routine of working six days a week, a few beers on Friday and Saturday, and church on Sunday. Once in a while, Lars and Frank would take the *Packet*, a regular scheduled boat that carried cargo, mail, and passengers to Winona and a train back to Minneiska. As with most new Minnesota towns, there were not a lot of single women

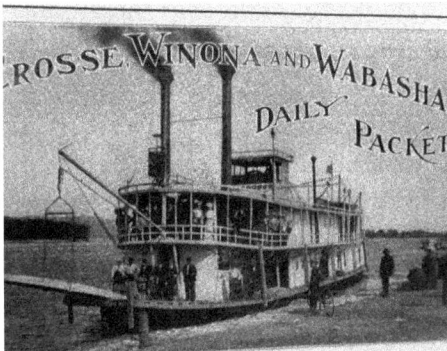

Lacrosse Wabasha Packet that stopped in Winona

around. Lars and Frank talked about the lack of women. That is why they would go to Winona monthly.

The letters to Gustava were a joy to write for Frank. It was almost like a diary. The letters summed up his month of activities. But he had to restrain himself from being too elated about his new life. The last letter from Gustava was nothing but sad news. She had closed the store in the fall of 1871. Katerina had left for Stockholm after the store closed. Katerina had met a military man and gotten married in Stockholm. Gustava was desperate; she had Peter Johan, who was only eleven, to take care of. She had no food. With the store gone, she had also lost the apartment above the store that she had been living in. All of Okna was in desperate straits. The despair was widespread in Sweden. She had no choice but to go to her brother Peter, on the Lindquist farm, and seek work for herself and Peter Johan.

Peter was his usual crabby self when Gustava came to the Lindquist farm. Peter and his family barely survived the famine. She asked for work for her son and for herself. Peter said yes. During the famine he couldn't feed the hogs and cows. So they had sold them off or eaten them. He would need extra labor to rebuild the farm. He had only three hogs and two cows left, and a couple of chickens. Peter showed Gustava the barn where Frans had lived. It was a stall converted to an apartment. Peter would get another bed for Peter Johan. Peter and his wife now had five children. Gustava would do chores in the house and gather eggs. Peter Johan would work with Peter around the farm. Gustava had never felt so sad, but what could she do? Gustava and Peter agreed to the terms. Gustava tried to make the stall in the barn more homey. But she realized it was still a barn. She signed the letter, "Love, Gustava."

Frank had tears in his eyes after he read her letter. He was sad for the Swedes that suffered so much, but especially for Gustava. Frank went on with his daily life. The new church was beautiful, and the building of the church was a way for the Swedes of Minneiska to grow closer.

Everything for Frank was going really well. The only thing missing was a wife. He was working on that. There were a few single women in the church. But the men outnumbered the women by two to one. He and Lars went to Winona more often now. He met a woman named Rachel on one of the journeys to Winona. The city was rapidly growing. Railroads and riverboats abounded. In 1870 Winona had more millionaires than any other city in Minnesota and was the third largest city in the state. Rachel and Frank's romance fizzled out after three months. He was settled in Minneiska; she was settled in Winona.

Then Frank got a real surprise. He got a letter from his brother Axel, who was two years older than him. Axel would be coming to Minnesota. He would take the same route as Frank and stop in Minneiska to visit. He had a job in St. Paul with the Great Northern Railroad. An agent had signed him up in Sweden and paid for his transportation. When Frank met Axel at the train station, they shook hands vigorously. They went to the saloon, where they visited for a few hours. Axel talked about Okna, how hard it was there, and Frank talked about how wonderful it was it was to be in Minnesota. Axel was jubilant. He realized he had made the right decision. He loved the trains and riverboats. Three days with Frank flew by, and he had to go to St. Paul. Frank walked Axel to the train station and said goodbye to his brother. Frank watched the train pull out of the Minneiska depot.

Lars announced that he was engaged to a woman he had met while building the church. Frank was again complaining to Lars about the lack of women in Minneiska. Lars responded that his sister, Josephine Olson, might be coming to Minneiska. Lars told Frank that Josephine would be perfect for him. That news perked up Frank. Frank prodded Lars to mention him in his next letter to Josephine. Frank pestered Lars for information on Josephine every time they got together. Finally, one day, Lars told Frank that Josephine was coming to America and would stop in Minneiska. If Josephine didn't like Minneiska, she would travel to St. Paul, where she had girlfriends that had recently immigrated.

In 1875 Josephine got off the train in Minneiska. Lars and Frank greeted her and welcomed her to Minnesota. Frank felt awkward, like a third wheel. Lars and Josephine talked nonstop. They hadn't seen each other in seven years. Finally Frank excused himself and went home. Lars and Josephine didn't realize he was gone. The next day, Frank worked all day and didn't see Lars and Josephine. Just as well. Because of a lack of eligible women, Frank was thinking of moving to Winona or St. Paul. His last hope was Josephine, and that was a failure.

A few days later, Lars and Josephine came into the hardware store at closing time. They asked Frank to join them for supper at their apartment. Frank readily agreed. Frank was soon talking to Josephine. The conversation flowed like honey. He was really smitten by Josephine. She had a lilt to her voice. Her voice drew him in to a place he had never been with a woman before. Lars made up an excuse and left and went to bed. They talked for hours. They discovered they had very similar dreams for the future. They had both made the arduous journey from rural Sweden to a new world. They both were excited for the future. They agreed to meet the next day. Frank couldn't sleep that night. He tossed and turned and thought of nothing but Josephine. He couldn't blow this. They met at the cafe for coffee. They both resumed the conversation from yesterday with the same intensity. Josephine said she had to leave soon to meet her friends in St. Paul. Frank froze. He was speechless. He stammered, "You can't go."

Now it was Josephine's turn to be shocked. She hesitated, then said, "I have to go to St. Paul; I will be back to visit Lars. I will see you then."

Frank was blowing it. He didn't know what to say next. He decided to keep quiet. Lars and Frank walked Josephine to the train depot and said goodbye. Frank mumbled something to Josephine. She didn't hear it. She boarded the train and was gone.

The next weeks were tough for Frank. He missed Josephine. He was morose and listless. The work days at the store dragged as never before. Next time he was out with Lars, they talked about everything except Josephine. A few weeks later, Lars and Frank met after work. Lars had a letter from Josephine. Josephine had found her girlfriends. She had gotten a job as a maid for a family on Summit Avenue. She shared an apartment with her three girlfriends on Dayton Avenue. She walked to work. She missed Lars and Frank and told them St. Paul was too big of a town for her. St. Paul's population was 20,000 in 1870, 40,000 in 1880, and 135,000 in 1890. It was growing too fast for Josephine.

Once a month Josephine would visit Minneiska. From her apartment in St. Paul, she would take a horsecar to the depot in downtown St. Paul and board a Milwaukee Railroad train to Minneiska. She enjoyed Minneiska. Visiting Lars and Frank was the highlight of the month. She made a few friends in town. When she was out with Lars and Frank one night, she requested that they look for a job for her. She was ready to move to Minneiska. Frank started looking the next day for a job. Jobs were easy to find in the booming economy of Minnesota. Frank found two jobs for Josephine, a maid's job and a store clerk's job. The next time Josephine came for her monthly Minneiska visit, Lars and Frank met her at the train depot. They went to lunch at the local cafe. Josephine talked excitedly about moving to Minneiska. Lars and

Frank had talked previously about the living arrangements. Josephine would live above the store with Lars, and Frank would find another apartment. Josephine thanked Frank for giving up his apartment. The weekend went fast, and it was time for Josephine to catch the train to St. Paul.

Lars checked on the jobs Frank had found for her. The maid job was all hers. She would start in a month. Lars wrote a letter to Josephine explaining the details of the job. Josephine replied right away that she would take the job. She took the train to Minneiska with all of her belongings, which fit in two suitcases. It was a new life, an exciting life. She lived with Lars and made new friends. She loved the Mississippi River and the riverboats. Daily she saw passenger riverboats, cargo riverboats, and log rafts pushed by riverboats to St. Louis.

She adjusted to Minneiska quickly. It was a much simpler life than St. Paul. The simplicity and beauty suited her. Lars, Frank, and Josephine were inseparable. The three of them took the *Packet* to Winona and the train back once a month. Frank suggested going to Wabasha, a river and railroad town seventeen miles upriver from Minneiska. That weekend was the grand opening of the Minnesota Midland Railroad from Wabasha to Zumbro Falls. It was a grand celebration, with dancing in the streets and food vendors. It was like a carnival. Minnesota Midland linked the towns along the Zumbro River to Wabasha, where a passenger could connect to St. Paul, Seattle, or Chicago. The year was 1878.

Frank and Josephine dated a few times. Josephine was reluctant. Frank was ten years older than her. But Frank persisted. His persistence paid off. Finally Josephine agreed to marry him. They set a wedding date of March 3, 1880. Josephine's three girlfriends would come from St. Paul, and they would be married in the Lutheran church in Minneiska. On the wedding day, Frank was ecstatic. He loved Josephine as much as he loved his new life in Minnesota. For Frank, his life was finally coming together. He had a wife that he loved and adored. They honeymooned in Wabasha at the Anderson House, a beautiful hotel built in 1856.

CHAPTER 2

St. Joseph, Missouri

St. Joseph, Missouri, known as St. Joe, was incorporated in 1843. It was a bustling outpost and a tough frontier town, serving as a jumping off point for settlers going up the Missouri River toward the wild west. It was the westernmost stop for railroads in America until 1869 when the transcontinental rail railroad was completed when the golden spike was driven in Utah on May 10, 1869. Jesse James was killed in 1882 in St. Joe. A decade later, Ben Peery was born in St. Joe in 1893. When Ben was twenty-one, in 1914, World War I broke out. He enlisted in the Army in October 1917. He went to basic training at Camp Funston, Kansas. After he finished

Buffalo Soilder.
Both the Patch and soldiers.

basic training, he was assigned to the newly created 92nd Infantry Division, which was an all-black Division. Before

the 92nd Division was deployed to France, the unit selected the American Buffalo as the division's insignia.

The Buffalo Soldiers had been formed in 1866 on the western frontier to fight Indians. The Indians nicknamed the soldiers "Buffalo Soldiers," because the soldiers' curly black hair reminded them of the hide of the buffalo. The 92nd Division motto was "Deeds not Words." The 92nd Division deployed to the Meuse-Argonne area of France, in the heart of the trench warfare with the Germans.

After World War I ended on November 11, 1918, Ben went back to St. Joe. He met Caroline Watson, and they married in St. Joe in 1921. Their first son was born on March 4, 1922, and they named him Ben Jr. The second child was born on June 21, 1923, and they named him Nelson. Ben Sr. was getting restless; he didn't make enough money as a construction laborer to feed his growing family. He saw a poster about the Postal Service hiring mail sorters on railroad cars. The Postal Service didn't discriminate; plus he got points for being a veteran. He took the civil service test and was hired by the Railway Mail Service (RMS).

The RMS had started between Chicago and Clinton, Iowa, on the Chicago Northwestern Railroad on August 28, 1864. The concept was a success. After that experiment, the operation was expanded to all railroads from Chicago. In 1869, the RMS was officially incorporated. The system expanded to virtually all the major railroads of the United States. The United States was divided into fifteen divisions. By 1907 over 14,000 clerks were sorting mail on passenger trains on over 203,000 miles of railroad. Over 10,000 trains carried mail sorter clerks The RMS would reach its peak in 1950.

Ben and another black man were hired in the seventh division, encompassing Missouri and Kansas, and head-quartered in St. Louis. The superintendent didn't want any blacks working in his division, so he offered a transfer to Ben to the tenth division, which consisted of North and South Dakota, Minnesota, and the Upper Peninsula of Michigan, headquartered in St. Paul. Ben could see he had no choice and cheerily accepted the transfer to the tenth division. He was assigned to Wabasha, Minnesota, as a base. They moved to Wabasha in 1928. They packed their suitcases and took the train to Wabasha. They found a house to rent on the Westside, where all the railroad people lived.

CHAPTER 3

Lengerich, Germany

The village of Lengerich, Germany, was founded in medieval times along the Ems River. It was always a marshy area, which kept the population sparse. The marsh extended sixty miles on each side of the Ems River. Lengerich lies 150 miles southeast of Hamburg and 60 miles east of the Dutch border. That was where Theodore Johan Roemer was born in 1803. His parents were Johan Roemer and Anna Engel Roemer. Theodore's parents were really surprised that Anna Roemer was pregnant. Johan was fifty-three, and Anna was fifty-one. Theodore was nine years younger than his older sister, Maria.

Unfortunately for Theodore, his parents both died in 1811, when he was only eight years old. The neighbors took him into their care, but he had to work for his room and board. Because he had to work the farm, there was no school for Theodore. He lived in the barn and worked from sunrise to sunset. His keepers fed him scraps of food. He ate in the barn. He was not allowed in the house. They always called him "boy"; he didn't think they ever knew his name. That was his life for eight years. Then, at sixteen, he ran away. He only knew he was sixteen because he had marked his age in the stall of the barn with a knife on his birthday. He went to the town of Lengerich and looked for work. He slept in the city park. He was uneducated and only knew how to farm. He hung out at the general store and chatted with the customers, looking for work.

Finally Bernard and Margaret Schmidt came to the store and were asking the store clerk if he knew of a boy that wanted work. The clerk called Theodore and introduced him to the Schmidts. Theodore went with the Schmidts that day to their farm a few miles out of town. He lived in the barn at the Schmidts', but ate supper in the house. After his last place, where he had worked like a dog and been treated like a dog, living with the Schmidts was heaven. The Schmidts were older, and their sons had farms and families of their own. Their youngest daughter, Adelaide, was still at home and was sixteen years old. Theodore never saw much of Adelaide, as she went to school in town and he worked all day at the farm. On Sundays Theodore would ride in the wagon and go the Catholic church with the Schmidts. Adelaide came along most Sundays. Sunday was a day of rest. After church they would spread a blanket on the backyard and pile the blanket with food. The neighbors would stop by and bring more food. Theodore had never seen so many sausages. The men would compare notes on the making of sausages and the various spices they would use. The conversation about sausages could go on all afternoon. Theodore felt at home, content, and part of the family. But at the same time, he felt restless. When he thought about the future, his future didn't include being a farmhand and living in a barn. But for now, he was content.

When Adelaide turned eighteen, she left for a job in town. She had a boyfriend who worked in the general store.

When Adelaide took an apartment in town, Theodore moved into her bedroom in the house. The Schmidts treated him like a son. He rarely saw Adelaide in the next several years. When he went into town with the Schmidts, he would talk to Adelaide when he saw her. Then Bernard Schmidt got sick. The doctor said it was consumption (TB). There was no cure. The only treatment was rest. When Bernard was bedridden, Adelaide moved home to take care of her dad. Adelaide moved into her old bedroom in the house, Theodore moved back to the barn. Theodore performed all the chores. He could handle the chores. He was thirty years old and used to hard work.

Theodore was aware of Adelaide. She had a presence and aura when she would be in the room that he couldn't ignore. He saw that she was gentle with her father and cared for him tirelessly. She never got crabby. At the end of the day, the two of them would sit on the porch and talk. That was Theodore's favorite part of the day. He realized he was missing something in life. He wanted to marry. He had never thought of marriage, because he had nothing to offer. He lived in a barn, was a farmhand, and had never been to school.

After Bernard died, he asked Adelaide for a date. She agreed. They went for a walk and held hands. It felt so natural. Adelaide stayed at the farm to look after her mother. They saw each other daily. At the end of the day, they would sit on the porch and talk. Not about the day's activities, but the future. They both wanted some future. Finally Theodore asked Adelaide to marry him. They set a date for September of 1835. He would be thirty-three and she thirty-one. Adelaide asked her mom if they could work the farm. Her mom readily agreed. They got married in the Lengerich Catholic church.

Theodore and Adelaide moved into the farmhouse. Theodore would work the farm, and Adelaide would take care of her mom. Theodore and Adelaide started having children. The first born was Bernard, born in 1836, named after Adelaide's father. Next was Joseph, born in 1839; following Joseph was Charles, born in 1842, and last was Mary, born in 1844. Adelaide was overloaded. She had four young children and her mother to take care of, plus the household chores. Theodore thrived on farm work. The more he worked, the happier he was. After church on Sunday, it was still a day of rest. They would spread the blanket on the lawn and pile it with food and beer. The neighbors would come over in the afternoon for the picnic. The beer would flow.

The conversation would focus on the troubles in the Kingdom of Hannover. Germany was not united then. It would still be a collection of kingdoms until Bismarck would unite Germany in 1871. The population was booming in Lengerich. There was not enough farmland, since it was mainly marsh. All the people of Lengerich had only one skill, and that was farming. The crops would fail once every couple of years. One Sunday, during the picnic at the Roemers' farm, a neighbor brought a booklet about traveling to America. Unlimited land was the lure. It got all the neighbors excited. Theodore talked to Adelaide that night about going to America. Adelaide couldn't leave her mother.

A few years later, Adelaide's mom got sick. The doctor came to the house and diagnosed Margaret's illness as TB. Adelaide knew how to care for her mom, since she had cared for her dad when he was dying of TB. Margaret died three months after she got ill. Adelaide notified her family members about Margaret's death. They had a funeral mass in Lengerich for Margaret. Then the family drama began. Adelaide's oldest brother, Carl, would inherit the farm. The custom in Germany was that the oldest son inherited the farm. Adelaide pleaded with Carl to reconsider the farm. Where would her family go? Carl said they could move into the barn and work for him. Theodore and Adelaide had no choice. They moved into the barn and worked for Carl.

Theodore explained to Adelaide that he was not settling for this. He wanted to go to America. Adelaide's mom was dead, and the family had no future in Lengerich. He started gathering pamphlets and talking to the neighbors. He settled on Iowa as a destination. Theodore had a decision to make as far as the route. He talked to two agents with pamphlets about going to America. One agent recommended taking a ship from Hamburg to New York, then a train to Chicago, then changing trains and going to Iowa. The second agent said the sailing to New Orleans was the only way to go. Also, New York had long delays for immigrant ships. Castle Garden immigration center wouldn't open until 1855. Ellis Island was just a dream; it would not open until 1892. If the Roemers would go via New York City, their ship could spend a week waiting for pier space. New York was a large city of six hundred thousand people. The Roemers could get lost in the hustle and bustle of New York City. Theodore decided to take a ship to New Orleans.

Money for the passage was a problem. He asked Carl for a loan. Carl could lend a little bit, but not enough for the whole passage. The neighbors added what they could spare, but in exchange Theodore would keep the neighbors updated on what life was like in America. The Roemers were set. Theodore booked passage with the sailing ship *Falcon* from Hamburg to New Orleans. The Roemers took a stage-coach from Lengerich to Lingen. Then took a new train from Lingen to Hamburg. It was the first time the Roemers had a ridden a passenger train. They couldn't believe how smoothly and fast the train could go. They had never been five miles from the farm before. The excitement was tremen-dous. Adelaide's heart was racing, and her body was in a cold sweat. Hamburg was overwhelming. They couldn't believe how many people lived in Hamburg. Lengerich was a vil-lage of four hundred people. They left the train depot and walked to the pier. They found their ship, the *Falcon*, and slept on the pier.

They departed on September 21, 1853. Theodore was fifty-two, Adelaide was fifty, and the kids ranged from nine to nineteen.

In the years from 1845 to 1855, one million Germans left their homeland to America. The Roemers were in the steerage class, as were almost all the Germans going to America. Steerage class was a level sandwiched between the upper deck and the cargo hold. The height of the steerage class was five feet and six inches. Each person was allotted a six-foot-by-two-foot area on the floor. There were no beds. The whole Roemer family of six was allotted a six-foot-by-twelve-foot area on the floor, for a crossing that averaged fifty-three days. The toilets were on the upper deck. A few buckets were scattered around the steerage deck when the toilets were closed during storms. Theodore got a bucket for his family.

Ventilation and light only came from the hatches when they were open. Rats scurried about. Urine, feces, and vomit smells were common. The diet of the passengers was sufficient to keep them from starving, but not healthy or appetizing. At the end of the voyage, the bread was moldy, the butter and pork rancid. The flour was full of bugs, and the water undrinkable. Disease was rampant on most of the crossings. Cholera, typhus, and smallpox were common. The worst killer of all was typhus, a lice-borne disease that affects victims' skin and brains, causing dizziness, headaches, and pain throughout the body. Typhus was nicknamed "ships fever." Those who died on the voyage were buried at sea.

The Roemers survived the crossing with only one storm. The storm lasted three days. During the three-day storm, nobody could use the toilets on the upper deck, because the hatches were closed. Everybody got seasick. The Roemers rolled back and forth on the floor with the ship's heaving. Nobody got up to puke in the bucket; They just barfed where they lay. They were rolling in puke, urine, and a little sea water that came from the hatch. They didn't eat for three days during the storm. Not that anyone wanted to eat. None of them had been this sick before. On day three of the storm, Adelaide wanted to die. She told Theodore to just throw her overboard into the ocean and let the sharks eat her. Luckily she couldn't get her wish. The hatches were bolted down, and nobody could get to the upper deck. Finally the storm subsided. The hatches were opened, and fresh air poured into the steerage deck. The Roemers gulped the fresh air greedily. They would all live. The rest of the crossing was uneventful. The moldy bread was just an annoyance, a petty thing.

When the Falcon rounded Florida, Captain A. J. Wade let the steerage class come onto the upper deck for the rest of the trip, because the Gulf of Mexico was smooth sailing. This was the Roemers' first glimpse of America. When the Falcon entered the Mississippi River to New Orleans, it was November 21, 1853, sixty days from their departure from Hamburg. They docked two days later in New Orleans. The Roemer family just walked off the ship. No customs, no inspection, and no paperwork was required. They were in America. They walked the levy and bought some food from a grocery store. They marveled at the French-style buildings in New Orleans, with their iron balconies. They ate their grocery store food in Jackson Square. Jackson Square had been renamed from Place D'Armes just two years prior when the statue of Andrew Jackson was erected. After lunch, they walked around New Orleans to get their land legs.

Later that afternoon, they went to the levy to find a riverboat to Iowa. They found a riverboat leaving the next day. They bought steerage class tickets and slept on the levy near the boat. The Roemers boarded the boat the next morning. The riverboat was a luxury liner, compared to the Falcon. They could stand upright and stroll the deck. They visited with other Germans going upriver. They found another family that they visited with a lot. They were from Lengerich. They excitedly told each other of their plans. The Mars family was going to Iowa because it had recently been made a state. Iowa had become a state seven years ago, in 1846. Theodore talked with his new friend, pumping him with questions on his plans. The Mars were getting off in Bellevue, Iowa, and were going to farm.

That night, Theodore talked with Adelaide about getting off in Bellevue also. She heartily agreed. She was tired of life on a boat. Plus, Theodore had a distant uncle who had settled in Bellevue. The Mars and Roemers got off in Bellevue. The Mars had someone to meet them; the Roemers had nobody. The Roemers did what they always did; they set up a camp on the Bellevue riverfront. A few days later, a priest discovered the Roemers camping and offered them to live in his parsonage. It was already December, getting cold, and the snow would be soon falling. The Roemers stayed for two months with the priest, on the second floor of the parsonage. The priest not only found Theodore's distant uncle, but a farm to rent a few miles out of town.

Theodore's uncle helped the Roemers find the farm and helped them move. The Roemers were finally settled on a farm and working at what they loved, farming. After a few years, the two oldest boys, Bernard and Joseph, were restless. They didn't want to work as farmhands for their parents. Bernard had taken the American name Ben and had just turned twenty-four. Joseph was twenty-one. Minnesota became a state in 1858, and the boys heard that Minnesota had plenty of farmland. They asked permission from their parents to go to Minnesota and strike out on their own. The parents agreed to the boys' request. Ben and Joseph took a riverboat and got off in Wabasha, Minnesota.

Wabasha's first settler had been August Rocque in 1826. Wabasha was named in 1843 after the great Dakota chief. It was incorporated as a city in 1858, the year Minnesota became a state. Prior to August Rocque were the French fur trappers and priests who had explored the upper Mississippi. Perrot, Fr. Hennepin, De LaSalle, Marquette, and Joliet had all had expeditions in the upper Mississippi River in the 1600s. Minnesota had exploded with settlers, going from 6,000 in 1850 to 173,000 in 1860. The Roemer boys worked for wages for a year. Then they could buy a 160-acre farm from Charles Read (founder of Reads Landing). They cleared the land and built a log cabin. They took a train to Bellevue, Iowa, in 1861 and talked their parents into coming to Wabasha.

The Roemers were still renting the farm in Iowa. Theodore was now fifty-eight years old and tired. They welcomed the move to Wabasha. They all moved into the cabin built by the boys in Wabasha. Theodore and Adelaide were finally settled. They had a 160-acre farm and house in Wabasha. Although there was no school for the Roemers to go to, they all could read and write German and English. The cabin was small and not big enough for six adults.

The next year, in 1862, the Roemers had a stroke of luck. The Homestead Act was passed. The Homestead Act was several laws passed in America; it allowed applicants to acquire government land. In all there were 160 million acres of public land; nearly ten percent of the total land in America was given away free to 1.6 million homesteaders. All three of Theodore and Adelaide's sons applied and got Homestead Act farmland in Wabasha. The daughter, Mary, married Ben Kennebeck, who had a farm in Wisconsin.

All of Theodore and Adelaide's sons got married and had children, except Ben. Ben never married and farmed by himself. He didn't trust banks, and all of his neighbors knew that. The rumor spread that Ben was wealthy and had cash in his house. On February 20, 1908, two men knocked on Ben's door, asking for directions to downtown Wabasha.

One of the men clubbed Ben to death at his front door. Ben had Emma, a twenty-one-year-old neighbor girl, cleaning the house at the time. She saw the men clubbing Ben to death and fled into the night and hid in a straw shock in the field. The two robbers looked for the girl and couldn't find her. They gave up and fled the scene. When the sun rose, Emma, who had almost frozen to death in the straw shock, ran home and called the sheriff. The sheriff came up empty handed. The cops never found the killers.

Theodore and Adelaide's son Charles had seven kids, six of them boys. There was no more good farmland in Wabasha, so Charles bought a farm across the river in Nelson, Wisconsin, in 1904. The German tradition of leaving a farm to the oldest son was still going strong. So Charles left the Nelson farm to his oldest son, Theodore. Besides being a great farm, the farm was situated upon the bluffs of Wisconsin. The farm had a great view of the Mississippi River and Wabasha. Theodore, after a short courtship, married the neighbor girl, Mathelda Markey. The wedding was in St. Felix Church in Wabasha on October 17, 1894. The first born was Carl, on October 19, 1897. The second child was Inez, born on May 16, 1899. The third was Linda, born April 27, 1904. The fourth child was Mae, born on May 23, 1915. And the last child was Leona, born on November 29, 1916.

August Stroot was born in Lengerich, Germany, in 1850. Many of his friends were going to America, especially to Wabasha, Minnesota. He was reluctant to leave Germany. He finally decided to leave when he was twenty-nine, in 1879. He boarded the ship *Strasbourg* from Bremen, Germany, to Baltimore. Then he took the Baltimore and

Ohio Railroad to Chicago and transferred to the Milwaukee Railroad to Wabasha. He had a lot of friends in Wabasha from Lengerich who had immigrated earlier than August had. He got a job as a farmhand. As in Germany, he lived in the barn. He met Theresa Jennings, who was twelve years younger, born in Germany in 1862. They married quickly on October 23, 1882, in Wabasha.

Because August was so late to Wabasha, the good farmland was already taken. He heard there was farmland in western Minnesota in the Bluffton area. He and Theresa bought an eighty-acre farm in the Bluffton area and started farming. They had seven children. The two youngest were twins, born on September 6, 1897. They were named Laura and Lawrence. Unfortunately for August and Theresa, there was a TB epidemic in the Bluffton area, and three of the firstborn children died young. Then one of the twins, Laura, died from TB at seventeen in 1914. This was too much for August and Theresa. The TB epidemic was killing not only their children, but the neighbors' children as well. They were panicking. They sent Lawrence to Wabasha to get him away from the TB pandemic. He was the youngest son. They had friends in Wabasha who could take care of Lawrence and get him a job as a farmhand. They never saw Lawrence again. Of August and Theresa's seven children, five died at a young age of TB. Another of the children died at thirty-eight in Bluffton. Lawrence, whom they sent to Wabasha, lived to be eighty years old.

Lawrence found a job as a farmhand in Wabasha. After four years of working for the same farmer, Lawrence was bored and wanted to change farms. He found a job across the river in Nelson, Wisconsin, at the Roemer farm. Theodore

Roemer's oldest child and only son, Carl, was leaving the farm to enlist in the Army for World War I. Theodore only had four daughters at home and needed a hired hand. Lawrence fit the bill.

Inez Roemer flirted with Lawrence, and a romance began. Inez would sneak into the barn where Lawrence lived. During Lawrence and Inez's romance, the Nineteenth Amendment to the constitution was debated and passed. It gave the woman the right to vote. When Tennessee became the last of the thirty-six states to ratify the amendment on August 18, 1920, it went into effect that day. Inez was thrilled at getting the right to vote; she painted

Lawrence Stroot and Inez Roemer on Beacon farm

on the inside of the barn on a piece of tin, "Inez, August 18, 1920," for all to see. Even on a remote farm in tiny Nelson, Wisconsin, women celebrated in their own way.

Lawrence and Inez got married on May 10, 1921. Inez was at least six months pregnant. She gave birth on July 29, 1921. They named the daughter Laura, after Lawrence's twin sister who had died at seventeen. Lawrence and Inez had eleven other children. Following Laura was Shirley, on July 7,

1923, Marge, on August 29, 1925, and Gene, on August 13, 1926. There was no room in the farmhouse, so Lawrence and Inez lived in the barn. Inez made a respectable home out of the barn. They stacked bales of hay around the stall, creating a wall and doorway. They had a horse blanket in the doorway for privacy and a horse blanket on the bales of hay that they had for a bed. It was a one-room home, but it was theirs.

Inez and her siblings, the children of Theodore and Mathelda Roemer had grown up during the infancy of aviation. The mail act of 1925 authorized the postmaster general to make contract airmail routes (CAM) with private commercial carriers, which would eventually create the airline system in the US. Thirty-four CAMs were authorized. Northwest Airlines incorporated in 1926 and was awarded CAM 9. CAM 9 was the route from St. Paul to Chicago by way of La Crosse and Milwaukee. The Post Office didn't want limits on mail delivery, so it built navigation beacons for overcast weather and nighttime operations. Starting in 1923, a system of rotating beacons was established on airmail routes. 1,500 beacons were built by the Post Office by 1933.

Northwest Airlines Mail plane and Bessie Coleman.

One day a stranger knocked on the Roemers' farm door and wanted to build a navigation beacon on the farm. Theodore agreed. The Post Office contractor started building the beacon in 1925. After the beacon was built, the Roemer farm was nicknamed the Beacon Farm. The beacon could be seen from forty miles away. Inez wrote a poem about the Beacon Farm:

THE LIGHT AT THE TOP OF THE HILL
When the shades of the evening gather, and the light in the West dies away,
I love to look over the river that ceaselessly flows on its way;
The valley is dark and silent, the river is deep and chill,
But constantly, cheerfully shining is the light on the top of the hill.

It is just from an unshaded window—the farmer has finished his toil.
The lamp on the table is burning, the coffee is beginning to boil;
No eavesdroppers near are intrusive, The beams shine as far as they will.
So over the Mississippi Valley shines the light from the top of the hill.

It shines for the father and mother; it shines for the babe on her knee.
It shines for whoever may see it; how often it shineth for me.

My eyes grow weary of darkness, are restless with
searching until
There flashes and gleams from the window, the
light on the top of the hill.

And then I look up in the heavens, to the stars as
they twinkle and shine,
Beyond the dark shadows of sorrow which cause us
to fret and repine
And I look for day that is coming, I think of it now
with a thrill,
When I shall cross over the river to the Light on
the Top of the Hill.

Inez started seeing airplanes flying overhead because
of the navigation beacon. Northwest Airlines started flying
mail from St. Paul to Chicago in 1926. Her interest grew as
she saw more airplanes overhead. She started reading about
Amelia Earhart, Bessie Coleman, Charles Lindbergh, and
Beryl Markham.

Bessie Coleman was born in 1892 to a family of share-
croppers in Texas. She saw her first airplane while picking
cotton at a young age. She got the aviation fever from then
on. She applied for several flight schools in Texas but was
rejected because she was black and female. Those rejections
didn't dissuade her. She applied for a flight school in France
and was accepted. She saved all her money and, with schol-
arships, graduated from Le Crotoy flight school in France.
On June 15, 1921, she got her international pilot's license.
She was the first black female to get a pilot's license. Bessie
returned to the US in September 1921 and began flying air

shows. She was soon nicknamed Queen Bess. She stalled her airplane and crashed in Los Angeles on February 22, 1923. She survived with a broken leg and three broken ribs. She saved all her money from the air shows and bought a Curtis JN 4 (Jenny). On her first flight in her new airplane, she crashed and died on April 30, 1926, in Jacksonville, Florida. She was only thirty-four.

The other pilot Inez read about was Charles Lindbergh. He was born in Detroit on February 4, 1902, and was raised in Little Falls, Minnesota. He bought his first airplane, a Curtis JN 4 (Jenny) and started doing airshows. When the Post Office started airmail routes, he went to work on CAM 2 from St. Louis to Chicago, flying mail in October 1925. This was good practice for his next adventure. He flew from New York to Paris on May 20, 1927. It was a 3,600-mile flight that lasted thirty-three hours. Inez was thrilled at Charles Lindbergh's accomplishments.

The other pilot that Inez followed was Amelia Earhart. Amelia was born in Kansas in 1897. She lived in St. Paul and went to St. Paul Central High School while her father worked for the Great

Amelia Earhart and below Amelia, Beryl Markham.

Northern Railroad. She died on July 2, 1937, on her flight from Howland Island to New Guinea. She was only thirty-nine years old.

The last pilot Inez followed was Beryl Markham. She was born in England in 1902 but soon moved to Nairobi, Kenya. She was a nonconformist. She married three times and had affairs with Prince Henry; Edward, Prince of Wales; and Denys Finch Hatton (Robert Redford in *Out of Africa*). She learned to fly in Africa and worked as a bush pilot. She spotted game from the air and signaled their location to the hunters on the ground. In 1936 she flew from England to North America nonstop in twenty hours. She was the first to fly from east to west across the Atlantic. She wrote of her adventures in the book *West with the Night*, published in 1942. She died in Kenya in 1986 at the age of eighty-three.

Inez tired of the farm life, the isolation, and living in a barn with a growing family. The Milwaukee Railroad was hiring across the river in Wabasha. Lawrence applied and got a job as a fireman on the steam locomotives, shoveling coal by hand into the boiler. It was a dirty and difficult job, but Lawrence was ready to leave the farm and live in a house. They found a house to rent on the Westside, near the depot and the grocery store. It was 1928. Their neighbors were the Peerys, who had recently moved from St. Joe, Missouri.

CHAPTER 4

Minneiska

Seventeen miles downstream, in Minneiska, Frank and Josephine Lindquist were starting to have children. The first born was Anna, in 1879. Following Anna was Mary, born in 1881. The third was Frances, born in 1883. Frances was the first glitch in Frank and Josephine's happy life. Frances was a sickly baby and died at three years old. Then Mabel was born in 1888. Frank was beaming. Everything had worked out beyond his expectations. He was forty-five years old, had a wife he loved and adored, had three young daughters, and lived in a land that knew no bounds. He lived in a beautiful town on the Mississippi River. He forgot about his hard life in Sweden. He never forgot Gustava, though. He still wrote her monthly.

One day when Frank came home, he found Josephine in bed. Josephine had never been sick a day in her life. She was ashen-looking and had a high fever. Frank summoned the doctor in town. The doctor asked Frank what Josephine's symptoms were. Josephine had diarrhea, nausea, and vomiting. The doctor gave Frank the sad news: it was probably cholera. At the time, there was a cholera epidemic in the US, especially in the upper Mississippi River valley. Josephine died on April 2, 1889. She was thirty-five years old. The US lost fifty thousand from the cholera in that epidemic. Frank was devastated. For the first time in his life, he broke down and cried. He had three young daughters; Anna was nine, Mary was seven, and Mabel was a baby.

The neighbors helped, but he needed a permanent solution. He wrote to Gustava. In the letter he told of Josephine's death. Frank pleaded to Gustava to come to America and help him raise his three daughters. As Gustava read Frank's letter, she cried. She missed Frank terribly. She hadn't seen him in twenty years. Gustava was living in a barn and doing chores for her mean older brother. She hadn't had contact with her two children since they had moved to Stockholm. Frank would pay for her passage to Minnesota, and she could start a new life. Not that she had a life in Okna, Sweden. If she didn't go now, she would never go. She lived a life of drudgery and sadness. If she went to Minnesota, she would never come back to her home in Sweden. She realized she didn't have a home in Sweden. She lived in a barn as a slave to her older brother. The decision became clear; she would go to America.

Frank set up her passage, the same route as Frank had taken. A stagecoach to Goteborg, a ship to Hull, England, a train to Liverpool, a ship from Liverpool to New York. Then take a train from New York to Chicago, changing trains in Chicago, and catching a Milwaukee Railroad train to Minneiska. Frank sent Gustava the details of the passage with English words to help her make connections. She boarded the ship *Romeo* in Goteborg on September 16, 1889. She was fifty-eight and was a gray-haired granny. She was doubting herself now as she scanned the other passengers, who averaged twenty-five years old. She would never see Sweden or her children again. She put that idea right out of her head and started talking to the other passengers. Their excitement lifted her spirits.

Frank's instructions were helpful, especially the Swedish-English translations. Her biggest challenge was changing trains in Chicago. Each railroad had its own train station. Chicago Union Station would not be built until 1925. She had to walk from the New York Central depot to the Milwaukee Railroad depot. She was exhausted. When Gustava finally boarded the Milwaukee Railroad train, she could finally relax. She had been traveling for

Passenger Train along Mississippi River. Probably Milwaukee RR train.

about forty days. The train conductor woke her up in Winona and told her it was about thirty minutes to Minneiska.

She was awed by the scenery. The train was hugging the banks of the Mississippi River. Riverboats were everywhere. When she stepped off the train in Minneiska, Frank was there to greet her. He had met every train for the last week. They hugged each other and cried tears of joy. In in that moment, Gustava realized she had made the correct decision. She hadn't felt this much joy in a long time. Frank and Gustava walked the block to his apartment above the store. When Frank opened the door, Anna and Mary were there to greet Gustava. The girls were hesitant at first. Who was this stranger entering their house? They all sat down for supper, and the conversation flowed. They talked in Swedish.

The girls could easily switch back and forth from English to Swedish. Gustava talked about her trip. New York City and Chicago were both too noisy and crowded. The beauty of the Mississippi River from La Crosse to Minneiska was like nothing she had seen before. Gustava was exhausted and went to bed.

Frank and the girls stayed up and talked about their new life. Frank explained to the girls that Gustava was their aunt from Sweden. She would live with them and raise them. They would be kind to her and not cause trouble. Frank was tongue-tied as he tried to explain to the girls that Gustava was not their mom but a replacement. He grumbled to himself as he realized that he was blowing it. He gruffly said, "Go to bed, girls." It was late, and it was past their bedtime. He would try another time to explain to the girls. He never had to explain to the girls about who Gustava was. The girls got on famously with Gustava.

They settled into a routine. Gustava got up early, made breakfast, and packed a lunch for Frank and the girls. Anna and Mary walked a block to school. Mabel was too young for school. After Anna and Mary left for school, Gustava cleaned the house, made the beds, did the laundry, and prepared supper. But most of all, she cared for Mabel. Gustava always hummed a Swedish song and had a sweet smile on

Lindquist Family in Minneiska, Back Row from left Anna, Frank, and Mary. Mabel in front row. Shortly after Josephine died.

her face while doing her chores. She truly loved the three girls. Gustava appreciated the second chance at life. She had a meaningful, rewarding life, and she knew it.

The girls grew up too fast. First Anna got married at nineteen. Anna married a boy from Minneiska who was six years older than her, named Charles Carl Johnson. Together they had four children, three sons and a daughter. They soon moved to St. Paul. Anna still took the train to Minneiska monthly to visit Gustava. Mary got married next, at thirty-two, in 1914. They stayed in Minneiska and had one son, who was named Rodney.

Mabel only knew one mom, and that was Gustava. Gustava taught Mabel to sew. At sixteen, Mabel went to work at the seamstress shop in town. Mabel still lived with Frank and Gustava in the apartment above the store. Gustava was now seventy-six, and Mabel eighteen. Mabel was doing most of the household chores when she got home from her seamstress job. That was Mabel's favorite time of day. Mabel would putter around the house, and Gustava would sit in the rocker and tell stories about her life in Sweden. About the famine, living in a barn, and the crossing of the Atlantic at fifty-eight. Gustava always finished with her story about raising three beautiful daughters on the American frontier. At the end of Gustava's story, she would smile and ask Mabel for a hug.

One day, Mabel was excited to come home and talk to Gustava.

Gustava and Mabel. Mabel was my grandmother

Mabel had met a man in the store. He was Swedish, had just arrived in Minneiska, and his name was August Nelson. Mabel thought Gustava was sleeping in the rocker, as she did a lot lately. Mabel went about her chores, trying to not disturb Gustava. Mabel realized Gustava was slumped in her rocker. She checked on Gustava, and she wasn't breathing. Frank came home, and Mabel met him at the door. Frank checked on Gustava and pronounced her dead. Mabel and Frank hugged each other and cried all night long. Gustava had lived in Minneiska since 1889, for over twenty-one years. Anna came from St. Paul and stayed with Frank and Mabel. Anna, Mary, Mabel, and Frank stayed up all night and told stories of Gustava. They all agreed they were the luckiest girls in the world to have Gustava in their lives.

The day of the funeral was a glorious day in Minneiska. There was the bluest sky the girls had ever seen. That was a sign that Gustava's spirit was looking down at them. Gustava would be their guardian angel and take care of them forever. Gustava is buried in Greenfield Cemetery in Minneiska. She never got back to Sweden or saw her two children ever again, but she lived a full life on the American frontier, raising three beautiful girls. The next day Anna took the train to St. Paul, Mabel went to her shop, and Frank went to the hardware store. Time marched on, but the girls had a huge hole in their heart that would last forever.

A year later Mabel was still sad about Gustava's death. She was lonely and still living with her dad. She was seeing more of August Nelson, who stopped by her shop several times a week. August got a job as a mailman in Minneiska, driving a mail wagon pulled by horses. He would deliver mail to the farmers. He would talk to the farmers about farm life and always asked if they knew of a farm for sale. He was frugal and saved his money to buy a farm. He was born on a farm in Sweden and loved the farm work.

Mabel and August's romance continued at a slow pace. He was reticent, and Mabel had to bring up the subject of marriage. August was reluctant to get married, because buying a farm was his first goal. Mabel was a city girl, and he assumed she wouldn't like farm life. He was wrong. She loved an adventure, and being a farmer was just another adventure. Finally, August heard of a farm for sale. He asked Mabel what she thought. Mabel said she would like to look at the farm. August hitched up the horse to the wagon, and they drove to the farm. Mabel loved the farm. The farm overlooked the Whitewater River and was so peaceful. August talked to the farmer, and after some negotiations, they agreed on a price. On the way home, August asked Mabel if she would marry him. She said yes. They set a date of Dec 29, 1915. August was thirty-seven, and Mabel twenty-seven. The house on the farm was small and simple, with three bedrooms upstairs and a kitchen, living room, and dining room downstairs. The house had no plumbing or electricity. The outhouse was near the house. They had kerosene lamps for light and, in the kitchen, a wood-burning stove for cooking and heat. August hurled himself into farming. He was a hard-working Swede, and the farm was all his. He felt wealthy.

Mabel started having babies. Sydney was first and was born in 1916. Lorraine was born in 1919, followed by Ronald, born in 1922. Then Frances was born in 1925, who was named after Mabel's sister, who had died at three years old. The last was Raymond, born in 1928. The boys slept in one bedroom, and the girls slept in the other bedroom.

One of the highlights was when the Watkins horse and buggy came from Winona, selling spices. The whole family would race to greet the salesman. For the farm families, who smelled cow and pig poop all year long, the smell of the spice wagon was a welcome relief. The wagon contained pepper, vanilla extract, cinnamon, ginger, clove, and peppermint extract. Mabel and her kids thought they were in heaven. Watkins was

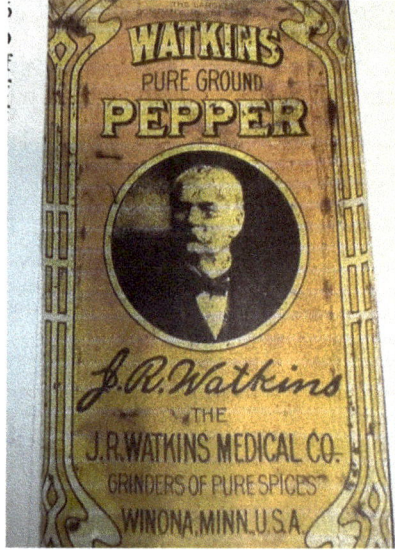

Watkins salesman and Watkins Label

founded in Plainview, Minnesota, in 1868. J. R. Watkins moved his company to Winona in 1885 because Winona was booming. During the World Wars, Watkins devoted ninety percent of their production to support the war effort. Watkins produced dried eggs, powdered juices, vitamin tablets, and hospital germicide during the war years. In 1940 Watkins would be the largest direct sales company in the world. Mabel always bought spices from Watkins from her egg money. Mabel, like all the farm wives, got to keep the money from the selling of the eggs. She got to spend her egg money any way she wanted, and she spent the money on spices from Watkins.

August didn't have a hay baler, so the three sons were needed during haying season. They walked along the hay wagon in the field with pitchforks, pitching loose hay into the wagon. The hay wagon was pulled by two Percherons named Doc and Silver. When the wagon was full, they had to load the hay into the hay mow on the upper level of the barn. They did this by hitching a horse to a fork that lifted the hay into the hay mow. There was a long rope attached to the release of the fork that, when pulled, would drop the hay wherever the farmer wanted.

Between crops August and his sons would clear more of the hillside land for fields. They would cut down the trees and then cut the trees into firewood for the kitchen stove. They would use dynamite to loosen the stumps and hitch Doc and Silver to the stump and drag the stump to the side of the field. They would burn the stumps the following year. Unfortunately

Nelson driving a hay wagon.

Doc or Silver pulling a stump out.

all the farmers were clearing the hillsides for fields in the Whitewater valley. That created annual floods, which devastated the small towns and farms. There were no trees or ground cover to hold back the rains from flooding into the Whitewater River. The devastation and degradation of the soils contributed to the valley's experiencing its first flood in 1900. Since that first flood in 1900, the Whitewater River was being flooded up to twenty times per year. Nelson's farm was high enough in elevation that it didn't flood. But all of the farms contributed to the flooding, including the Nelsons'.

Low-lying fields and houses were buried under fifteen feet of eroded sand and silt. The towns of Beaver and Whitewater Falls were eventually abandoned. Elba, which stood on higher ground, only survived from recently built dikes. In 1938 the Whitewater River flooded twenty-eight times. Sometime in the 1930s, the Issac Walton League of Minnesota petitioned the Conservation Corps to establish a game reserve in the Whitewater Valley.

Richard Dorer started working for the Conservation Corps in 1938 at the age of forty-eight. He had been born in Ohio in 1889 and had attended West Point. He was a classmate of Dwight D. Eisenhower and served in World War I as an infantry captain. He was awarded many medals for his bravery, which included a Purple Heart, two French War Crosses, and a Silver Star. But he was best known as a conservationist who saved the Whitewater Valley. On his first visit to the Whitewater Valley, in 1938, he could readily see the destruction of the valley. He was a man of action and began purchasing farmland as the state administrator of federal wildlife funds.

In 1943 he purchased thirty-eight thousand acres along the Whitewater River. Values of the farmland were dropping because of the erosion and flooding. The farmers were happy to sell. As an example, a ridge farm purchased in 1916 for $16,000 was sold in 1946 for $4,000. FDR established the CCC (Civilian Conservation Corps) in 1933 to combat the depression. The CCC built lots of dikes in the Whitewater Valley. The Soil Erosion Service (SES) taught farmers how to contour farmland, how to do strip cropping, and other conservation measures. Both the CCC and the SES, along with Richard Dorer's actions, saved the Whitewater Valley. Dorer died in 1973 at the age of eighty-four and is buried in the land that he cherished and saved. He is buried in Beaver Cemetery, in the town that was abandoned. The million-acre forest all around Beaver Cemetery is named Richard J. Dorer Memorial Hardwood State Forest.

The reasons farm boys dropped out of school at sixth grade was that they were needed on the farm. Thus August Nelson didn't need a hired hand; he had three sons who could work the farm. Girls were not needed for farm work, so Frances didn't drop out at sixth grade. She loved school and wanted to go to Winona High School after sixth grade. Mabel thought education for Frances was a waste of time as well as an inconvenience. Daily, August would have to hitch Doc to the wagon and drive Frances to the bus stop which was two miles away. After a lot of pleading from Frances, Mabel relented and allowed Frances to go to Winona High School.

Frances tested out of seventh and eighth grade, so got into high school after she finished sixth grade in the one-room school by the farm. Thus she graduated from Winona High School at only sixteen in 1941. After high school, Frances wanted to see more of the world instead of farm life. She talked to Mabel about Milwaukee and St. Paul for business school. Mabel made the decision for Frances. She could go to St. Paul, because Mabel's sister, Anna, was in St. Paul. Frances wrote a letter to her aunt Anna. Anna wrote back saying that Frances was more than welcome to stay with Anna. Her kids were grown, and Anna had an empty bedroom. August hitched Doc to the wagon and took Frances to the Milwaukee depot in Minneiska. Frances boarded the train to St. Paul and settled in with Anna.

CHAPTER 5

Depression

Ben and Nelson Peery were adjusting to their new home on the Westside neighborhood of Wabasha. The boys' parents, Ben Sr. and Caroline, were adjusting as well. The parents loved shopping at the Westside Grocery Store and Tavern. Ben Sr. would have a beer at the Westside Tavern and got to know the regular customers of the tavern. He felt welcome. The bar talk centered around the railroad. The Peery's immediate neighbors were Inez (Roemer) and Lawrence Stroot and their children, Shirley, Marge, and Gene.

The Stroot and Peery kids grew up on the West Side during the depression. The West Side was little more than a railroad junction where dirt-poor farmers brought their cattle, wool, and cabbages to the Westside railroad yard for shipment to St. Paul. Nelson Peery was quoted as saying,

If a kid had to grow up during the depression, Wabasha was as good a place as any. It was obvious the Peerys were black. But where people are all poor, it didn't matter whether someone was black, Polish, white, or Mexican. They had everything they needed in walking distance. There were two grocery stores,

Maggie's and Westside. The Westside store had a tavern also. There was a school and the Milwaukee depot, where the men walked to work. During the Depression there were only three automobiles on the Westside out of a hundred households. They didn't need cars; everything was within walking distance. The houses had large yards for the kids to play in. If the yards were not big enough, the railroad had a large ball field by the depot. The town whistle blew at noon and at 6:00 p.m. Nobody had watches, and all the Westside kids had lunch at noon and supper at 6:00 p.m. When the whistle blew, the kids dropped everything and ran home. They wolfed down their food and raced out the door to play baseball or Kick the Can. There was no washing of hands, napkins, salad, or dessert. The meal consisted of a piece of meat, a canned vegetable, and potatoes. The kids would play outside till dark, when they would go home to bed. Before bed, the kids would get down on their knees and say their prayers. Every household said the same prayer. "Now I lay me down to sleep, I pray the Lord my soul to keep. God bless Mommy, Daddy, Grandma, and Grandpa."

During the school year, the Westside kids would walk to the two-story public school a few blocks away. The first four grades were on the first floor. Grades five to eight were on the second floor. On each floor there was a row of chairs for each grade. Miss DeWitt taught all eight grades. She would teach the row of first graders first. Then she would move to the second row of seats and ask them to recite their homework. When Miss DeWitt moved to the upper floor for grades five through eight, the first floor was supposed to do their assignments.

Halloween with kids from Westside school with Ben Peery (third from right) Building, Westside school.

Nelson Peery was sitting next to Shirley Stroot during the first day of school. Shirley introduced herself and asked his name. He replied, "Nelson Peery, and I am your neighbor."

"Nelson," Shirley said, "my mom said you ain't no different from nobody else except God kept you in the oven too long."

Nelson that thought that God didn't keep Shirley in the oven long enough. Nelson and Shirley became good friends from that day onward. When Shirley visited the Peerys the first time, she was surprised when Nelson introduced her to his grandma Molly. Shirley's grandma still lived on the farm and did daily chores. Shirley couldn't fathom Molly sitting around the house all day. From then on, Shirley visited the Peerys almost daily. She loved listening to the stories of Nelson's grandma. Molly told of her father being a slave in Horse Cave, Kentucky. Molly also told of stories of the Civil War. Another favorite story of Molly's was how after the Civil War, she traveled in a covered wagon to Kansas.

Kansas was the great frontier, and there were opportunities for black farmers there. Shirley loved listening to Molly's stories, even if Molly repeated the stories numerous times. Molly died in 1949 in St. Paul, Minnesota. She was eighty-one years old and had stories to fill a book.

The stock market crashed in October 1929. That didn't affect the Westside families at first. They all kept their jobs. They were poor and still happy. Life was as simple as before the crash. The kids walked to school, and the dads walked to work. They had enough food to eat. The kids still played baseball and Kick the Can. The whistle still blew at noon and 6:00 p.m. Then in 1933, the Dill Company in town shut down, the Big Jo Flour Mill went part time, and the Milwaukee Railroad started laying off workers. Lawrence Stroot was one of the railroad workers laid off. Ben Peery Sr. was not laid off, because the mail had to be delivered. The Westside kids noticed there were more kids in St. Joseph Orphanage. St. Joseph Orphanage had been founded in 1900 when Bishop Joseph Cotter of Winona placed four orphans in Wabasha in the care of the Sisters of Sorrowful Mother. In 1904 the Winona diocese started building an orphanage on the Westside, which included an elementary school. It was dedicated in November of 1905, when Bishop Cotter walked from St. Felix Church to the St. Joseph Orphanage on the Westside. Eight hundred people attended the ceremony.

Bishop Joseph Cotter had been born in Liverpool, England, in 1844. When he was five, he immigrated to America with his parents. The Cotter family spent time in New York and Cleveland before moving to St. Paul, Minnesota. He became a priest and attended St. John's Seminary as a student of theology. In 1889 Pope Leo XIII appointed Joseph Cotter as the first bishop of the Diocese of Winona. Bishop Cotter was a strong supporter of the National Temperance Movement. He travelled throughout the country lecturing on the evils of alcohol. He received sixty-nine thousand pledges from peo-

ple who promised to give up alcohol. He died in 1909 at the age of sixty-four. The Catholic school founded in Winona in 1911 was named for Bishop Cotter.

St Joseph Orphanage on Westside.

Most people think of orphanages as homes for children whose parents have died. During the Depression poor families who couldn't feed their kids gave up one or two of the kids to the orphanages. One example was Anna May Strub, born in 1918 in Ryegate, Montana. Her mom died in 1919, when Anna May was only one year old. She had eight older brothers and sisters. Her dad raised the kids by himself until he got remarried in 1929. His new wife didn't want to raise so many of his young kids. So he put Anna May on a Milwaukee Railroad train in 1934 to Wabasha, Minnesota. She entered St. Joseph Orphanage on the Westside. She went to St. Felix High School and married Floyd Riester in 1939. They lived on the Westside, across from Westside Grocery Store.

The orphanages were overcrowded during the Depression, especially in New York. The nuns in the New York orphanages wrote letters to the nuns in the Midwest, asking if any farm families could adopt orphans. The only stipulation for the nuns in New York was that the orphan had to complete sixth grade. Mathew Drees was born in New York in 1913 and was given up for adoption. He was only six years old when the Kohn family, a farm family near Wabasha, replied to the nuns at the St. Joseph orphanage. They would adopt young Mathew. He came from New York on a train with twenty other orphan kids and one nun. The orphan train stopped in Wabasha. Mathew stepped off the train, and the Kohns were there to greet him. He went with the Kohns to their farm. He had a new life in a new family, in a strange place, as a farmhand. Mathew, a boy from New York, had never seen a farm before.

He finished sixth grade as the New York nuns demanded. He lived with the Kohns and was a farm hand until eighteen. At eighteen he left the Kohns, adopted their name, and became a truck driver for Bub's Beer out of Winona. He finally got a Bub's beer distributorship for all of Wabasha County. He died in 1961 when his beer truck ran off a rural road. St. Joseph Orphanage was a tough place to grow up. During the summer months, the orphan kids would work ten hours a day in the garden. The St. Joseph Orphanage had a huge garden and grew their own food. The orphan kids canned the vegetables and placed the potatoes in the root cellar. The orphan kids would play with the Westside kids.

Lawrence Stroot got a job as the only cop in Wabasha when he was laid off from the Milwaukee Railroad in 1933. There was nothing but petty crime in Wabasha. It was an easy job until Bonnie and Clyde robbed a bank in southern Minnesota. The stories of Bonnie and Clyde's criminal adventures captivated a downtrodden nation at the height of the Great Depression. Their outlaw antics and unlikely love story helped turn the gangsters into folk heroes like Robin Hood and Maid Marian.

All the police in southern Minnesota were on alert. Bonnie and Clyde could overwhelm any police force in rural Minnesota. They had a lot of fire power. Their arsenal included numerous shotguns, three Browning Automatic Rifles (BAR), and thousands of rounds of ammunition. Lawrence Stroot, the only cop in town, had a very small 38 pistol. The Texas governor, Ma Ferguson, appointed retired Texas Ranger, Captain Frank Hamer, to hunt down Bonnie and Clyde, dead or alive. Frank Hamer was credited with fifty-three kills of bad guys and had suffered seventeen wounds to his body.

Henry Methvin was part of the Bonnie and Clyde gang. His father, Ivan, made a deal with Louisiana Sheriff Henderson Jordan who passed the info to Frank Hamer. The deal would be that Henry would be paroled if Henry's father gave the rendezvous spot of Bonnie and Clyde. Ivan parked his truck on the rendezvous spot with a flat tire. Captain Hamer, with five lawmen, set up an ambush on the rendezvous spot on Louisiana Road 154 on May 23, 1934. The plan worked perfectly. Bonnie and Clyde slowed down to assist Ivan in changing his tire. The six officers fired 130 rounds into the car, killing all of the occupants. Lawrence Stroot couldn't be more relieved. He didn't have to worry about Bonnie and Clyde robbing a bank in Wabasha.

Meanwhile more hobos were showing up on the doorsteps of the families on the Westside. The estimate was that there were four million hobos traveling in boxcars, looking for work or food during the Depression. Of that number, 250,000 were teenagers. The universal symbol for a house that was kind to hobos was an X. Ben Peery noticed an X on the fence to their house and talked to his mom. He wanted to erase the X, but Caroline Peery said no, leave it. Ben knew all of the families from the Westside were going through hard times. He knew his family was struggling, with barely enough to eat. He was confused. Caroline said, "We have to take care of those in need."

Caroline often invited the Negro hobos to dine with them. Ben remembered a Negro hobo, Ned, with a southern drawl, from Louisiana. Ben loved listening to Ned's stories of the cities he had seen, all by boxcar. Ned was very cordial. After supper the conversation lasted for an hour or so. Grandma Molly told stories about Kentucky with her father born into slavery. Caroline talked about St. Joe, Missouri. Ned would talk about his travels and the cities he had seen. Caroline gave Ned a sandwich when he left. Ned was grabbing the next freight train south. Ben asked, "Where will you sleep?"

Ned said, "A sidecar pullman"—which was hobo speak for a boxcar.

The Depression was getting worse. The Rail Mail Service enacted a pay cut to all of their employees. Ben Sr. started coming home drunk. One night Ben and Nelson were home when their dad staggered home from the Westside Tavern and Grocery Store. Caroline chastised him for being drunk in front of the boys. Ben and Nelson just snickered. Half of the Westside families were without work. Ben Sr. was fortunate that he still had a job, even though at reduced pay. When the neighbors came to the Peerys' front door looking sheepish and mumbling to Caroline, Ben and Nelson would see their mom reach in her purse and give the neighbors a few coins. As far as Caroline was concerned, this was what neighbors did for each other.

Ben and Nelson knew that the family didn't have enough food, so they started stealing from the railroad. They would walk to the freight yard and find a boxcar that was easy to get into. Ben and Nelson convinced themselves that taking apples and corn wasn't stealing. A person had to eat, after all. Caroline looked the other way when the boys brought home food. They needed the food. Ben and Nelson fished more than ever now. The slough was nearby, and with their cane poles, they would catch as much fish as they could take home. Sunnies, crappies, and bullheads were plentiful. Caroline poured the coffee grounds on a patch of dirt in the back yard that became a worm farm. The worms loved coffee grounds.

One day when Ben and Nelson were looking for food in the boxcars, they saw a group of official-looking men with shotguns. Ben and Nelson hid from them and watched what they were doing. In the freight yard, there was a pen for cattle that were waiting for shipment to St. Paul. They watched in awe as the men shot the cattle, poured bags of lime on the dead cattle, and covered them with dirt. A few Westside men cursed at the federal agents. The agents retorted that this was the only way to come out of the Depression. One of FDR programs was the Agriculture Adjustment Act (AAA). The price of cattle and pigs dropped precipitously during the depression, putting farmers into bankruptcy. This was the government's solution to stabilize the livestock prices. Less supply equals higher prices. The Westside families couldn't see the purpose of the program. They were starving, and the agents shot the cattle. The cattle could have fed all of Westside for at least a year. Six million pigs were killed and buried under the AAA program, enough to feed 600 million people one meal. The US only had 123 million people during the 1930s. The amount of pigs killed during the AAA program could have fed each person for a week.

During recess one day at school, Ben and Nelson were in a tussle with another classmate. Miss DeWitt questioned Ben and Nelson. "Who started the fight?"

They both declined to answer. Then Miss DeWitt asked the class who started the fight. Shirley Stroot squealed on the boys to Miss DeWitt. Shirley said Ben and Nelson had started the fight. Ben and Nelson plotted how to get revenge on Shirley. They knew Shirley's route home, because they were neighbors. They raced ahead of Shirley and hid in a ditch. When Shirley came abeam their hiding spot, they jumped up and scared her. She ran home crying. When Ben and Nelson came home, they knew they were in trouble. Mom was crying, and Pop was angry as all get out. Shirley's father, Lawrence, had called Ben Sr. and complained about Ben and Nelson scaring Shirley. Ben and Nelson's hearts were pounding, and they understood what they had done.

Ben said, "We didn't hurt her. She snitched on us, and we just scared her."

Pop said, "My God, boys, aren't you ever going to learn? You are Negros in an all-white town."

Pop reached for the heavy leather gun belt. Mom left the room. The boys received their first real beating. Pop said, "I will beat you half to death before you make another Scottsboro case in Wabasha."

Pop called Lawrence and said to him, "Yes, I gave them the worst whipping they ever received. I hope we can keep this between ourselves. No, I am sure they didn't mean any harm. They will be all right. They have to learn someday, or they will get killed. They would like to apologize to Shirley."

Pop handed the phone to Ben first. "Beg her pardon," said Pop.

Ben said, "I am sorry, Shirley." Then Ben handed the phone to Nelson, and Nelson apologized to Shirley. The boys were sitting on the floor and bawling now. Pop left the room, and Mom came back, her eyes swollen and red from crying.

"Boys, I am sorry you got such a whipping. But we've tried to tell you a thousand times to stay away from the white girls. Leave them alone. White boys can do a lot of things that you can't. I want you to listen to me! You have to conduct yourself so that everyone forgets you are Negro. Don't ever forget that."

A few days later, everything was back to normal. Shirley came after school to visit the Peerys and talked to Grandma Molly about her tales in Kentucky and her covered wagon ride to Kansas. The boys played Kick the Can with the neighbor kids. Pop went on his ten-day trip to Walla Walla, Washington and back.

The reason Ben Sr. and Caroline were concerned about Ben and Nelson was because of the Scottsboro Boys. On March 25, 1931, black and white teenagers were traveling in a box car from Chattanooga to Memphis. There was a fight between the blacks and whites; the white teenagers lost the fight and went to the sheriff, complaining they had been attacked by a group of blacks. The sheriff got a posse and arrested the blacks. Two young white girls riding in the box car were also taken to jail. The two young white girls accused the blacks of rape. The trial took place in Scottsboro, Alabama, in a rushed trial. All nine of the black boys were convicted of rape and sentenced to death. The Communist Party of USA (CPUSA) defended the black boys pro bono. The US Supreme Court ordered a new trial. The new trials were moved to Decatur, Alabama. The medical examiner testified that there was not a sign of rape in the young white girls. The court convicted the nine blacks of rape again. Most of the convicted blacks served six to thirteen years in prison.

Clarence Norris was the only one sentenced to death. His death sentence was commuted in 1938 by the governor of Alabama. He was paroled in 1946, fifteen years after the trial. He violated his parole, moved to Brooklyn, New York, got married, got a job, and had children. In 1976 he was caught in New York for parole violation and sent to prison. Then Governor George Wallace pardoned Clarence in that same year. Every black family in the US had heard of the Scottsboro boys. Ben Sr. and Caroline Peery had certainly heard of the Scottsboro boys and didn't want that to happen to Ben and Nelson on the Westside. They had a close-knit community on the Westside and didn't think it would happen in Wabasha. But then again, it only took one angry father to get the ball rolling.

Ben had an interest in airplanes. He built model airplanes from kits made of balsa wood. The engine was a rubber band attached to a propeller. He got all the Westside kids interested in model airplanes. Ben started a model airplane club. They would meet on Saturdays at the Peery house and work on building the model airplanes. They would share techniques of building model airplanes. On Sunday the kids would fly the airplanes that they'd built the day before in the depot park. They would see how far their airplanes could fly. Ben's model airplane went the full length of the park, about one hundred yards. He was the winner of the longest-flight contest. Building and flying model airplanes amused the Westside kids for years.

When Ben Sr. was on one of his ten-day trips to Walla Walla, there was a Fathers and Sons banquet in town. The Episcopal church in Wabasha had a minister named Father Calhoun. Father Calhoun was childless and was truly fond of Ben and Nelson. Father Calhoun asked Caroline if he could take Ben and Nelson to the banquet. At the banquet, Father Calhoun introduced Ben and Nelson as his sons. After the banquet, Nelson became an acolyte in the Episcopal church, and Caroline was so proud.

One night at supper, Ben announced he had a girlfriend. Grandma Molly snickered, and Pop was outwardly calm, except for dropping his food from his fork onto his lap. Pop said, "Well, that is fine, Ben. I guess you are man now." But Pop gave Caroline a look that said, "We have to talk."

Pop called the girlfriend's mom. The mom said that it was just puppy love and was cute. She had no problem at all with them dating. Pop and Caroline didn't see eye to eye on this issue. Caroline thought it was fine. The Westside was their home. She liked it here. Pop said they now had seven sons, three born in Wabasha, and the problem wasn't going away. It might be fine that Ben was dating a white girl, but the six other boys could have problems. Pop won the argument. Pop wrote a letter to the district supervisor requesting a transfer to St. Paul. He laid it out brutally in the letter. He had seven sons, and the oldest, Ben, was a freshman in high school. He lived in an all-white town. There were no other blacks anywhere near Wabasha, much less in town. He desperately needed a transfer to St. Paul. Within a month the transfer was approved.

The day of the Peerys' move, the Westside neighbors came to help load the truck. The women cooked enough food to feed an army. The doctor who had delivered three Peery sons, the sheriff, and Fr. Calhoun all came to say goodbye. The kids stood sadly around, making their final goodbyes. A few tears were shed by adults and kids alike. Shirley gave Nelson a big hug and a kiss. She would miss him and never forget him. Finally the truck was loaded, and it was time to go. Ben and Nelson rode in the truck with Pop. Caroline and the other five boys walked to the depot and boarded a train to St. Paul.

As Ben and Nelson left Wabasha, their hearts hurt. They would never live this type of life again. Ben recalled in an interview, reminiscing about his life in Wabasha, "It was a very happy life. We were the only black family in town, but it didn't matter we were black. We knew we were black, just like every Polish family knew they were Polish. It just didn't have that kind of structuring role in our lookout. We were just a part of the community, a very tight-knit community. It was the age of innocence. A very marvelous way to grow up."

Ben went to the University of Minnesota, majoring in physics, then Fisk University in Nashville for a master's degree, and the University of Michigan for a PhD in astronomy. Later he was the chairman of physics and astronomy at Howard University. Nelson Peery was an author who wrote eight books, including *Black Fire*, which he tells the story about growing up in Wasbasha. Ben died in 2010 in Silver Springs, Maryland, at the age of eighty-eight. Nelson died in September 2015 in California at the age of ninety-two. Their mom, Caroline, died in 2000 at the age of 106. They had lots of stories.

CHAPTER 6

World War II

L ife started improving on the Westside. The US started coming out of the depression in 1940. FDR's programs were working. Lawrence was hired back to the Milwaukee Railroad. Most Westsiders got their jobs back. There was plenty of food on the table again. The Peerys were missed, especially by Shirley. Because of the declining number of orphans in the Westside orphanage, the Winona Diocese decide to close the St. Joseph Orphanage. The remaining orphans were going to move to the orphanage in Winona. The Westside orphans were going to miss their friends, their wonderful neighborhood, and their school. The Westside was the only home they knew. They complained to St. Joseph Orphanage staff. Winona Orphanage didn't have enough beds for all the Westside orphans, so the diocese came up with a plan. The plan was to pay a small stipend to any Westside families who could take in orphans. Inez (Roemer) Stroot took in an orphan named Richard, whose father had died in railroad accident, and his mom couldn't afford to raise him. Richard would go to the University of Minnesota and become an MD. Once again, the Westside took care of their neighbors.

Then in a surprise attack, Japan bombed Pearl Harbor on December 7, 1941. The US entered the war the next day. Congress lowered the draft age from twenty-one to eighteen on November 11, 1943. Most of the Westsiders enlisted in the armed forces. They were patriotic, and they had a duty to defend their country. Shirley's brothers, Gene Stroot and Don (the younger), visited the Wabasha Draft Board on Monday, December 8. Don entered the navy at seventeen, and Gene entered the Marines at eighteen. Don was assigned to a Navy Seabee outfit building runways on islands in the South Pacific. After basic training in Parris Island, Gene was assigned to an aircraft carrier as an antiaircraft gunner.

Another boy from the Westside was Luke Howard Beaver. He was born in 1926 and entered the Army Air Force a month before graduating St. Felix High School. He was a B-17 tail gunner in the South Pacific. After the war, he stayed in the air force and entered pilot training based in Barstow, Florida. He died when his training aircraft crashed in a cypress swamp. He was married to Gloria, a daughter of Linda Roemer, who grew up on the Beacon Farm in Nelson, Wisconsin.

In Minneiska, on the Nelson farm, August and Mabel's oldest son, Sydney, was twenty-five on December 7, 1941. He enlisted in the army and went to basic training as the oldest man in basic training. After basic training, he was selected as a machine gunner on a jeep. He was deployed to England and landed on Normandy Beach on D-Day. The most dangerous part of Sydney's job was crossing the French hedgerows in a jeep. The Germans would wait for the jeeps to cross the hedgerows and pick them off. Finally, the army figured out a solution. They attached snowplows to the front of the tanks. The tanks would clear an opening in the hedgerow for the jeeps and soldiers to go through. During the British and American bombing runs, Sydney and his army buddies would stop and look up in the sky in awe. The number of bombers would darken the sky. Sydney had never seen an airplane before World War II, much less the waves of bombers going overhead.

Sydney's unit was attached to Patton's 3rd Army during the Battle of the Bulge. He was wounded and recovered in a French hospital. He rejoined his unit in time for the liberation of Paris. He was a farm kid from Minneiska and had never seen a city like Paris. He rode down the Champs Élysées on August 29, 1944, in the victory parade. The female Parisians were kissing the American GIs. Sydney got his share of the kisses. Even though Sydney had gotten wounded and some of his buddies had been killed, marching through Paris was the biggest thrill of his life. After the war was over, Sydney went back to Minneiska and got a job as a mailman. He drove the same mail route that his father had done, delivering mail in a horse and buggy.

Matt Metz entered the Army Air Corps in 1942. After advanced training, he served as a B-24 tail gunner. He was based in Foggia, Italy. On his thirteenth mission

Matt Metz

on, February 13, 1945, his airplane was shot down over Yugoslavia. He was a POW for two months in Stalag 13. He was liberated by Patton's 3rd Army in April of 1945. After the war, he came back to Wabasha and served as the county agent for Wabasha County. Sydney Nelson's unit was attached to Patton's 3rd Army when they liberated Stalag 13. They never knew they lived seventeen miles apart. There are too many stories of the boys from the Westside who fought for their country to name here.

When Carl Roemer returned from World War II, he got a job as a bartender at Westside Tavern next to his sister Inez (Roemer) Stroot. Carl was discharged from the Army in 1943. He had been wounded in the leg, and the leg never healed. He had a permanent limp. He lived with his sister Inez. The owners of the Westside store were Henry and Katherine Briggs. Henry Briggs died in Feb of 1945. Carl started dating Katherine Briggs soon after Henry's death. They married on January 9, 1946. Carl then added a dance hall to the Westside Grocery Store and Tavern. It was a huge success. The boys were coming home from World War II, and they wanted to party. Overflowing crowds filled the dance hall every Saturday night.

About this time, Frances Nelson came home from Minneapolis to visit her brother Sydney and her parents, August and Mabel. Sydney suggested they go to Wabasha to a new dance hall he had heard about. Frances met Inez's son, Gene Stroot, at the dance. Gene was just recently discharged from the Marines and lived next to the Westside Tavern with his mom. Sydney met Maureen Holland, a farm girl who had been given up by her parents to the St. Joseph Orphanage during the Depression. They danced up a storm. The war was over, and all the people were celebrating. There was optimism in the air. The Depression and the war were over.

Gene, Francis, Maureen, and Sydney felt that they had never known a normal life. They had only been six years old when the Depression had hit; then they'd fought in World War II. This normal was new to them. They liked this normal and were celebrating. Gene and Frances's romance went quickly. They married on November 22, 1947. Sydney and Maureen's romance went slower. They were married in 1951. Like his dad, Lawrence, Gene was hired by the Milwaukee Railroad as a fireman and was based in St. Paul. Frances worked for the Peavy Grain Exchange, and after they were married, they rented an apartment in Minneapolis. Terry was born in January 1949 in Minneapolis. But Gene and Frances didn't like the big city to raise children, so they moved to Wabasha and rented a house on the Westside. Gene got a transfer to Wabasha, and Frances quit her job to raise Terry.

They finally found a small farm to buy. It was still on the Westside and included an old farmhouse, a small barn, a silo, a chicken coop, and ten acres. They didn't have enough for a down payment, so Frances asked her dad for help. August Nelson agreed to lend them a down payment. August still believed farmland could only go up in value. They moved into the farm. Mike was born in January of 1951. Terry and Mike lived a very carefree life, like the previous generation on the Westside during the Depression. The town whistle still blew at noon and 6:00 p.m. Lunch and supper were at noon and 6:00 p.m. All the kids dropped everything and ran home when the whistle blew, wolfed down their food, and ran outside to play with the neighbor kids.

During the summer Mike and Terry had their cane poles and worms for bait, and they fished daily. They caught sunnies, crappies, and bullheads. They had a rowboat in the slough below their house and could row the boat anywhere. The slough emptied into the Mississippi River, and they could go into the river, but they tended to stay in the slough. The fishing was better in the slough. Mike and Terry had a large yard and laid out a ball field. The neighbor kids, Ray and Brian and Jim and Billie, always played in their yard. There was a streetlamp in the corner of the yard, where they placed the can for Kick the Can.

Because the farmhouse was old, with no insulation or storm windows, in the summer it was really hot in the second-floor bedrooms. So the boys put up a tent in the backyard and camped in the tent for most of the summer. They would chop wood for the fire they had almost every night. The boys would gather Frances's empty hairspray cans all winter and toss the cans into the fire at night and watch them explode. They were careful and would duck their heads behind a good-sized log.

Every Sunday after church, the family would visit Frances's parents, Mabel and August, at the farm. Mike and Terry were fascinated that Mabel's farmhouse didn't have electricity or plumbing. In the summer when it was wet after a rain, the Stroot car would get stuck in the mud. August Nelson would hitch up Doc and Silver and pull the car out of the mud. The boys peed behind a tree instead of going in the outhouse, which really stunk. At sunset, they would go home to Wabasha. The Nelsons went to bed at sunset and got up at sunrise. They had kerosene lamps that would give a little light, but not enough when it was good and dark.

When the DNR of Minnesota finally bought the farm, Mabel and August bought a farm a couple miles away. But the new farm didn't have a house. No problem for the Nelson family. Every weekend, they would all gather to build a house. Nobody in the family had built a house before, but they were young, strong, and confident. Mike and Terry would go with the family to watch the house being built. They watched in awe how fast the house went up. Mike and Terry soon got bored with watching the house being built, so they played in the barn, gathered the eggs for Mabel, and teased the pigs.

When the house was complete, the Nelsons bought their first tractor and retired Doc and Silver to the pasture. It took a summer to build the house. Since it was a house with plumbing and electricity, Mike and Terry spent a week each summer with Mabel. August Nelson had died shortly after the house was built. Spending a week on the farm with Mabel was like going to camp with no rules. Mabel didn't pay attention to what the boys did during the day. She rang a bell at noon and 6:00 p.m. for lunch and supper. The boys ran to the house and wolfed down the food and ran outside to play. The favorite activity during the week was playing in Trout Creek. The boys built a dam from rocks to form a lake. It worked for a few days, and the power of the water moved the rocks, and the dam broke.

Mike and Terry always had a dog at home, a mutt. The dog never slept in the house, maybe on the porch when the temperature was below zero. All the dogs were named Charlie. The dogs loved to chase cars, especially the mailman's car. Once every couple years, the dog would get too close to the car, and the car would run over the dog's leg. Dad would come home to a dog that was in pain. Gene would toss a piece of meat to the dog and shoot the dog in the back of the head with his shotgun. Mike and Terry would grab their shovels and bury the dead dog in the pet cemetery. One day the dog was hit by the mailman's car, and dad was away for the night for work. The Stroots had a renter in the house named Jim. Jim had a bow and arrow for hunting, and he volunteered to put the dog down with his bow. He missed the dog's head, and the arrow went through the dog's lungs. Mike and Terry stared in disbelief as the dog ran in circles, yelping and barking in pain. Jim grabbed Gene's shotgun and shot the dog. Mike and Terry, with tears in their eyes, grabbed the shovels and buried another dog in the pet cemetery.

Mike and Terry raised rabbits as well. The boys had cages for the rabbits and let them roam during the day when they could watch them. The rabbits loved the clover in the grass. The boys also supplemented the rabbit's diet with rabbit pellets. It took twelve months for a newborn rabbit to reach adulthood. The boys had dozens of rabbits. Mike started naming the rabbits. That was a mistake, because Mike got attached to the rabbits that he named. He thought of them as pets. Dad would come out of the house and say to the boys that it was time for rabbit stew. Dad would grab a rabbit, and Mike would protest, "You can't take that rabbit—that is Lucy."

Dad would say to Mike, "Then you pick a rabbit."

Mike picked Leo. At the supper table, Mike was tearing up. He was eating Leo. From then on, Mike only named the dogs, not the rabbits. The rabbits were just food, like squirrels.

The boys also raised chickens, had a couple of cows for milk, and a couple of pigs. When the family butchered the chickens, Dad would cut the chickens' heads off with a hatchet. Then the chickens would fly headless. The first time Mike and Terry saw the chickens fly headless, they were gobsmacked. After supper the family would clean the chickens on the same table that they just had supper on. Dad tried every method of cleaning chickens. The one that worked the best was dipping the chicken in hot wax. Mike and Terry would pull the big feathers off and pass the headless chickens to the younger siblings, who, with a tweezer, would pluck the pinfeathers. Dad would then cut up the chickens, place them in plastic bags, and freeze them for future use. They butchered chickens at least three times a month.

One Christmas Mike and Terry got bikes with a front basket on them. The bikes were heavy, single-speed Schwinns. The boys usually got their underwear, socks, and T-shirts wrapped up as gifts. Fran and Gene liked a Christmas tree loaded with gifts for the kids. So they wrapped anything that the kids needed during the year. The boys knew it was a special Christmas with bikes as a present. That was a real game changer, as the boys could double the miles they could travel from home. The bikes were pure freedom. That next summer they could bike to Third Cave, Coffee Mill Cave, and across the dike road to Nelson. The favorite thing the boys would do was bike up the Hump (Highway 60). The Hump was at least a six-hundred-foot hill. The boys would love to bomb the hill. They would start at the top of the hill and pedal with all their might and speed down the hill. They could pass cars that were doing 25 mph. It was a real thrill.

Mom loved that the boys had bikes, as she couldn't drive. Mike and Terry biked to the Westside store to get what was on Mom's shopping list. Uncle Carl was now the owner of the Westside, because of his marriage to Kathy Briggs. Carl charged the groceries to Gene and Fran's bill. Gene and Fran tried to pay the bill off at the end of the month, but they never could. Carl carried the balance without interest. That is how the Westside was. You took care of the neighbors in need, just like Caroline Peery had done during the Depression, handing a few coins out to the neighbors and feeding the hobos.

One summer, Gene was working in Winona and switched the Ringling Brothers Circus train all day. The Ringling Brothers Circus was playing Winona for the weekend, and they were just setting up. The Ringling boss gave four tickets to Gene for

Ringling Brother elephant

his effort on switching the circus train. When Dad got home from Winona, he asked Mike and Terry if they wanted to go to the circus tomorrow night. The boys were so excited. Mom had to stay home to take care of the younger kids, so Gene invited his sister to go. The family went early and had great seats. The show was an amazing display of colors, high-wire acts, animals, and music. Ringling had a three-ring circus under the big top, so there was action nonstop. Mike and Terry had never seen anything like this before. They were dazzled. The parade of performers and animals at the end of the show was magical.

The next day, Gene told the boys the circus train was going by the house to St. Paul. Mike and Terry walked to the tracks and waited. While they waited, they put a few pennies on the track to see how the train would crush them. Dad told them there would be two circus trains; the first train would be all the flat cars, with the circus wagons and the animals in cages. The second train would be the passenger cars and sleeper cars, where the circus people lived. Mike and Terry counted ninety-nine cars on the first train. They saw elephants, horses, tigers, lions, and lots of circus wagons. They had just seen the circus the night before under the big top, and now they saw it up close all packed up going to St. Paul. As the first circus train passed by, they looked for their pennies. The pennies had fallen off the tracks, but they found them nearby. The pennies were really flattened and almost twice their original size. The boys could hear the second train whistle, and they scampered off the tracks. The second circus train came by, and it was boring. Nothing but sleeper cars and passenger cars. That was the only time Mike and

Terry saw the Ringling Circus, but it left a lasting impression.

Every summer the *Avalon*, a paddlewheel boat, would visit Wabasha for one day. It was a special occasion for all the people in Wabasha. Even if you didn't buy tickets for the *Avalon* cruise, you would go to the riverbank and watch the *Avalon* arrive and depart. The *Avalon* had been built in 1914 in Pittsburgh. It was built for the West Memphis Packet company and was initially named the *Idlewild*. It was used as a passenger ferry between Memphis and West Memphis, Arkansas. The *Idlewild* was sold in 1947 and was renamed the *Avalon*. It became a tramp steamer, operating on the Mississippi, Ohio, Missouri, Tennessee, Cumberland, and St. Croix Rivers. The *Avalon* needed only five feet of water before running aground, so it could navigate almost any river in America.

Ringling Brother pics. Bottom pic, Cap from Avalon

The *Avalon* had two distinct cruises: a day cruise for families and a nighttime dance cruise for the adults. The *Avalon* would connect two cities and board passengers for a round trip. For example, the *Avalon* would depart Wabasha about

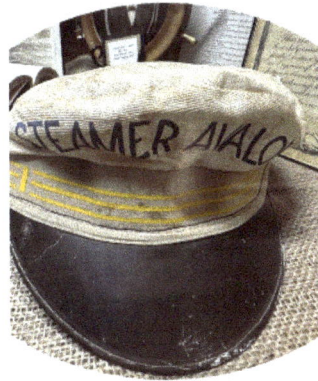

noon for the family excursion and cruise upriver to Pepin, Wisconsin. They would pick up passengers from Pepin and return to Wabasha fully loaded. The *Avalon* would then drop off the passengers from Wabasha and return to Pepin and drop off the Pepin passengers. It would sit for a couple hours in Pepin and reconfigure for the night cruise. The *Avalon* would board passengers in Pepin about 7:00 p.m. and cruise to Wabasha, where it would pick up the passengers for the night excursion to Pepin. It would drop off the Pepin passengers and return to Wabasha. They would drop off the Wabasha passengers and move to the pickup town for the next city pair.

The *Avalon* had a great dance floor and a superb dance band. The family would park on the riverfront. The boys would watch the *Avalon* park, drop the gangway, and board the passengers. The steam calliope

Avalon

would be playing all the time. The boys liked the nighttime the best, because the *Avalon* would depart with her lights ablaze, like an elegant birthday cake moving upriver and the sound of the calliope carrying in the wind. Short cruises were a dying business. The *Avalon* was sold in 1962 to the city of Louisville. It was renamed the *City of Louisville* and still does cruises today.

The other excitement for the summer was the Wabasha County Fair. The carnival would set up on the downtown streets. The Wabasha County Fair also had an outdoor stage that had live music every day. The bands were local country bands and rock and roll bands from the Twin Cities as head-liners. Mike and Terry would walk downtown to the fair and hang out all day at the fair. The carnival rides, the music, and the farm animals kept the boys

Wabasha County Fair

entertained all day. One summer Mike and Terry walked downtown early Thursday morning when the carnival arrived to set up. They hung around the carnies, looking for work. The boys got jobs working on the Ferris wheel. Mike and Terry were given passes for the carnival rides in lieu of cash. From that time onward, when the carnival came to town, the boys would go downtown early and wait for the carnies to hire them.

Since Mike and Terry had seen the Ringling Brothers Circus in Winona and the Ringling Circus train, they pestered Gene about other circus or carnival trains going by the house. One day Gene told the boys that the Royal American Shows train was coming by in two hours. The boys excitedly went to the track, waiting for the train. Royal American Shows was the midway for the Minnesota State Fair in St. Paul. It had been founded by Carl Sedlmayr in 1923 and was privately owned. It toured state fairs in the US and western Canada. Royal American Shows had won the contract with Calgary for the Calgary Stampede in 1934. That contract made Royal American Shows the king of the carnival circuit. Royal American Shows employed Lash LaRue, Gypsy Rose Lee, and Sally Rand (fan dancer). It even hired Colonel Tom Parker in 1931. Colonel Tom Parker sold candied apples, met his wife at the carnival, and was exposed to the cultural and political dynamics of the South and Midwest. He had been born in the Netherlands and entered the US illegally in 1927, when he was eighteen years old. He met Elvis in 1955.

Mike and Terry soon saw the train coming. The first train carried all the midway rides and animals. The second train carried the carnies in sleeper cars and coaches. In 1967 Royal American Shows was carrying eight hundred employees in the second train. Every summer the boys would watch for Royal American Shows trains coming by the house.

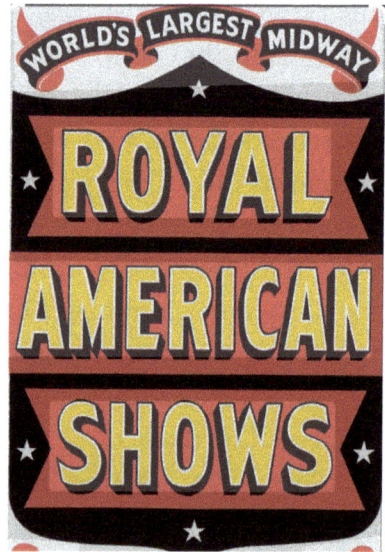

Royal American Show emblem.

Between the big events of the summer—the *Avalon*, the country fair, and the circus trains—they fished, played baseball, and explored the countryside. The families from the Westside never went out to eat. That was too expensive. For a treat during the summertime, Gene and Fran would load the family into the car and drive them to the A & W root beer stand. Back then, the A

& W stand had car hops. The A & W root beer stand would have small root beer mugs for kids. That was enough for the kids. They only drank water and milk all year round, and root beer was too much for them. They would drink the root beer down quickly, and foam would come out their nose. Carbonation and sugar were too much for the kids.

Mike and Terry's neighbors were Ray and Dar Passe. Ray Passe was the local mailman. To supplement his income, he would trap muskrats. Mike and Terry were interested in making money. Ray taught the boys how to trap pocket gophers and muskrats. Trapping gophers was the perfect summer activity. The boys bought traps and started trapping gophers. They got twenty-five cents a gopher. All the boys did was cut off the front feet and put them in a coffee can filled with rock salt. The boys did not just trap on their ten acres, but the neighbor fields as well. In the fall they would take their gopher feet to Virginia, the city clerk, for the bounty. Virginia would always empty the coffee can with gopher feet on her desk and, with a pencil, would count the gopher feet. Usually the boys trapped about 180 gophers per summer, for which they got forty-five dollars in cash from Virginia. The boys were rich. Mike started trapping muskrats in the slough, skinning them, and stretching the skins on a wire frame. The buyer of the skins would come in late fall and, with a little haggling, agree on a price. The price was usually about one dollar per skin. Mike trapped about a hundred muskrats per season, at a dollar per skin. He was wealthy.

One November day Terry was walking home from school after sunset, and he heard Mike screaming for help. Terry ran as fast as could to the first house, which was Ray and Dar Passe's. Terry ran into the house and told them Mike was screaming for help. Ray ran out of the house and tore through the trees to the slough. Dar ran to the rowboat and rowed to the sounds of Mike's cries. Terry was amazed that the Passes could run that fast at their age. They were probably only in their late thirties. Mike was stuck in the mud, and his boat had drifted away. Ray and Dar rescued Mike. Mike was chilled to the bone and was turning blue. When Ray and Dar got Mike to his house, Mom and Dad ran a hot bath and put Mike in the tub. He thawed out.

———

Gene was German Catholic, and Fran was Swedish Lutheran. They were not allowed to have a wedding in the St. Felix Catholic Church. They had a civil ceremony for their wedding. They decided to raise their kids Catholic and send them to St. Felix parochial school. Fran Stroot believed in getting the finest education available. St. Felix didn't have a kindergarten, so Fran sent Terry to the kindergarten at Wabasha Public School. The Wabasha Public School didn't have bus service for Catholic families. So Fran hired the only taxi in town, run by Roy Hopkins, to take Terry to kindergarten.

Roy had been born in 1896. He worked stamping buttons out of clam shells for the Wabasha Pioneer Pearl Factory. He later became a union representative for the same company. The first job of the clammers in the Mississippi River was to look for pearls. The leftover shells the clammers sold to the button factories. Clamming was a thriving business in the upper Mississippi River. The button factories would stamp out buttons from the clam shells. Roy Hopkins worked stamping buttons until the clam buttons were replaced by plastic in 1940. When the Wabasha Pioneer Pearl Factory shut down, Roy started a taxi company in Wabasha. That's who Fran called to take Terry to kindergarten.

Roy was a bachelor and lived in a shack with the bare essentials. He did not have indoor plumbing, so he didn't shower in the winter. Terry rode the taxi to kindergarten daily. He always hung on the passenger door to get away from Roy's stench. One day, coming home from school, the passenger door flew open, and Terry was flung out of the taxi. He was scraped up on his arms, legs, and face. Fran asked, "What happened to you?"

Terry replied that he had fallen out of the taxi. Fran got out the trusted Mercurochrome and wiped the cuts from Terry's fall. Mercurochrome would be banned in the US in 1998 because of the mercury in the product. After Fran cleaned Terry up, he went out to play with the other kids till the whistle blew at 6:00 p.m., when all the kids ran home to supper. When Gene came home, he called Roy Hopkins, and the two of them came up with a solution. Next day Roy's taxi was in the driveway at the appointed time. Roy opened the driver door for Terry, and Terry slid into the taxi. He noticed the passenger door was wired shut with baling wire. A Westside simple solution. Roy never fixed the door. Terry finished Kindergarten riding in Roy's taxi every day.

The following year Terry entered St. Felix Catholic School as a first grader. The teachers were Notre Dame nuns whose headquarters were in Milwaukee. The headquarters had been founded when Mother Mary Caroline Friess arrived in Milwaukee in 1851. With funding from King Louis of Bavaria, Mother Mary had established the first motherhouse of the School Sisters of Notre Dame in America. Milwaukee was only five years old and had a population of twenty thousand people when Mother Mary arrived. It was a rough-and-tumble frontier town. The mission of the School Sisters of Notre Dame was to provide education for the poor. Mother Mary also founded Mount Mary College for women in Milwaukee. Mount Mary was the first four-year Catholic college for women in Wisconsin.

Meanwhile in Wabasha, Father Felix Tissot founded St. Felix Parish in 1858, the same year Minnesota became a state. In 1874 he wrote a letter to Mother Mary of Milwaukee requesting she send nuns to teach in his newly opened St. Felix school. Mother Mary sent Sister Mary Venantia and Sister Mary Saturnina to St. Felix School in Wabasha for the start of the school year in September of 1874. The two sisters started teaching eighty-seven students. The students were fifty percent white and fifty percent Indians. Seven years later the student body more than doubled to 185 students. That made St. Felix a well-established school. The German heritage of the Notre Dame sisters was felt even in the 1950s. At the end of the day, the nuns would play marching songs by John Philip Sousa so the students could march out of school.

In 1933, when the Nazis came to power in Germany, they not only persecuted the Jews and Gypsies, but the Catholics as well. The Nazis shut down Catholic churches and the Catholic schools. The Nazis sent three thousand priests to Dachau Concentration Camp, of whom one thousand died. The time after the war was no better time for the Germans, especially women. Two million German women were raped by Russian soldiers. Starvation was widespread. German women had few options. One option was to join a convent and go to America.

The School Sisters of Notre Dame got a few German nuns because of their German heritage, and a few nuns got assigned to St. Felix. The students noticed that a few nuns had German accents. The German nuns taught German as a foreign language. It was popular class. Every Friday during German class, the nuns would lead the students in bawdy German drinking songs. Mathew Kohn, the beer distributor, dropped off a keg of Bubs beer to the nuns weekly.

One fall day, Mike came home with a baby goat he had found in the slough. Mike named the goat "Billy." Billy ate everything: clothes from the clothesline, all the flowers and vegetables from the garden, and even tin cans. Goats are very curious and just nibble on tin cans and clothes. They don't really eat them. Finally

Billy the goat

Mike and Terry built a pen for Billy because of the damage he was causing around the yard. The pen for Billy started a new adventure for the boys. The boys could ride the goat like a bucking bull. The boys started a rodeo with Billy and the Westside kids. The object was to ride the goat for the longest time. All the Westside kids tried to ride Billy. They always got bucked off. The crowd would cheer for Billy. The rodeo was a hit for the Westside kids. There were larger and larger crowds for the daily rodeos. When a kid got bucked off Billy, he had to run for it, as Billy was not done with the rider. Billy would lower his head and try to ram the rider. The crowd cheered for Billy, of course. All the Westside kids thought they could ride Billy. That was delusional; nobody could ride Billy.

The boys realized the rodeos were getting boring. What they liked was seeing the kid running from the goat as Billy tried to ram the kid. The boys would sucker little boys into seeing the goat, and the boys would toss the little boy into the pen and watch Billy charge him. The boy would run as fast as he could to the fence with terror in his eyes. The boy never made it to the fence, The goat always got him. Soon the neighbor kids would not stop by, because they knew what would happen to them. The boys turned to little brother Rich, as he was always home. Rich would be walking by, and the boys would grab him and toss him in the pen. Rich never beat the goat. Rich got wise and stayed away from the boys. The boys had no one else to toss in the pen. Once in a while, cousins would come to visit, and they always wanted to see Billy. The boys would toss the cousins into the pen. Since they were new to the game, they never had a chance to outrun Billy.

The fun stopped when mom came home one day when Billy was out of the pen. Billy rammed Fran against the garage, spilling her groceries. That night Gene made a few calls and found a taker for Billy. Next morning Mike and Terry walked Billy to his new home. The boys hugged Billy, and Billy knew his life had changed. The fun was over for Billy, Mike, Terry, and all the Westside kids. The boys walked home with tears in their eyes. They would always miss Billy. At least the boys didn't have to bury Billy in the pet cemetery.

One summer day there was a picnic put on by the Milwaukee Railroad in the park by the depot. There were hot dogs, ice cream, and races for the kids. The funniest race was the three-legged race. One leg of a girl and one leg of a boy were tied together with twine. They raced for about fifty yards. It took a lot of coordination. Boys and girls at eight years old had no coordination. Most teams tripped and fell down. Laughter came from the all the railroad families watching the race. During the middle of the picnic, somebody shouted "Fire!" The Stroots' barn was burning. Fran and Gene rushed off to the fire, leaving the kids at the picnic. They knew the neighbors would take care of the kids. When Fran and Gene got home, there was nothing they could do. The barn was gone. The two cows and all of the pigs were burned up. The chickens were fine, because they were in the chicken coop next door to the barn. The fire department did a good job of saving the chicken coop.

The Stroot family missed the cows the most. The family drank over two gallons of milk per day. The dilemma was how to replace the milk from the cows cheaply. Gene asked around, and he heard

Hay mow

the Bruegger farm sold milk directly to families. Gene bought a three-gallon pail, called the Brueggers, and arranged the milk pickup. After supper the whole family would pile into the car and drive to Brueggers. The Brueggers would be doing the milking when the family arrived, so the boys would play in the barn haymow. As far as Mike and Terry was concerned, the Bruegger barn was another playground. The Brueggers had a long rope in the haymow. The boys would scramble up to the rope in the rafters and swing over the hay. The boys would let go of the rope and fall into the loose hay. The drop was about fifty feet. They couldn't get enough of the rope swing. From then on Mike and Terry always went on the milk run.

Gene would drop the boys at Grandma Stroot's (Inez Roemer) to watch TV on Saturday. This was Mike and Terry's first exposure to TV, because their parents couldn't afford a TV. The boys' favorite shows were westerns. They always watched *The Lone Ranger*, *Roy Rogers*, and, their favorite, *The Adventures of Wild Bill Hickok*, with Andy Devine as Jingles. The other show they would watch was *Sky King*. When the boys were watching *Sky King*, Grandma Inez Stroot would take a break from her chores and watch with the boys. Inez would tell stories about her life as a kid on the Beacon Farm. Inez told about watching Northwest Airlines airplanes fly over the farm on the mail routes to Chicago. Growing up on Beacon Farm, she had been fascinated with airplanes. She saw airplanes daily. She would tell the boys about Lindbergh crossing the Atlantic from New York to Paris in 1927. Then she would talk about the woman pilots. She would tell about Amelia Earhart trying to fly around the world and disappearing in 1937, then Queen Bess flying airshows and crashing and dying in 1926, the year Gene was born. And lastly she talked about Beryl Markham, who was raised in Africa. Beryl flew solo from England to Nova Scotia. Mike wasn't paying attention to Grandma's stories; he would rather watch westerns. Terry loved Inez's stories about aviation, and Mike loved watching westerns. Once in a while, Mike would mimic Jingles and say, "Hey, Wild Bill, wait for me!" Mike got really good at imitating Jingles. A few years later, Gene and Fran got a TV. That ended the Saturday with Grandma Stroot and her stories. In retrospect, it was a sad day when the boys got TV. Terry loved Inez's stories just as Shirley liked Grandma Molly's stories of traveling in a covered wagon to Kansas.

Once a month, the Westside men would gather in someone's garage for a booyah. A booyah is a type of thick stew particular to Minnesota and the upper Midwest. The men from the Westside never had a recipe; they experimented every time. They would have a booyah kettle and create a broth and throw in carrots, onions, peas, and potatoes. After the broth was simmering, they would add some meat that they had hunted in

Booya Kettle

the past week. The meat could include squirrels, chickens, rabbits, turtles, and even muskrats. There was always a keg of beer, and the beer would flow. It was like making sausage on the Roemers' farm in Germany. In Germany, every man had an opinion about what spice should be added to the sausage, and in Minnesota, what meat should be added to the booyah. The conversation would flow as well as the beer all afternoon, about the makeup of the sausage in Germany or the booyah in the Westside.

There was a municipal garbage dump in town. Wabasha, back then, didn't have garbage pickup. Each household dropped their garbage off at the dump. Cars constantly got stuck in the mud of the dump. That was why Gene Stroot hitched a trailer to the Farmall Cub tractor. The family dumped the garbage in the trailer till it was full. The boys went along with Gene on the garbage runs. They also took their .410-gauge shotguns to shoot rats. The rats were everywhere. Nobody cared if the boys with shotguns shot rats in the dump in the center of town. Gene secured the lower part of the boys' jeans with a thick rubber band so the rats wouldn't climb up the pant legs of the boys.

After Gene dumped the garbage, it was time for a little scavenging. The boy were shocked what people threw away. Perfectly good things that just needed a little repair. Most times the boys would come home with a load of really good stuff. The boys would clean and repair the items, and they were as good as new. Gene got tired of the dump runs, so he taught the boys how to drive the Farmall Cub. The boys would do the dump runs alone, without Gene. You didn't need a license to drive a tractor. On the first dump run, Mike didn't put the clutch in when he started the Farmall Cub. Unfortunately, the Cub was in gear and in the garage. Mike crashed through the garage door. Mike didn't get hurt as the garage door crashed on his head. The boys tried to repair the garage door before Gene got home, but to no avail. Gene was not angry; stuff happened when you let boys be boys. Mike learned a good lesson though. Always check if the Farmall Cub was in gear, or step on the clutch. One time on one of the dump runs, little brother Rich wanted to ride along and shoot rats. He stood on the hitch and fell off the tractor. Mike didn't stop. Rich was running between the tractor and the trailer, trying to not to get run over by the trailer. Finally Mike gave Rich a hand as he clambered onto the hitch and made it safely to the dump. Rich didn't go on another dump run.

Another chore was gathering wheat from the railroad yard. Gene would hitch up the trailer to the Farmall Cub, load a few shovels and several gunny sacks, and head to the railroad yard with the boys riding in the trailer. Back then wheat was carried in boxcars, with boards inserted in the door opening to keep the grain in. There was always leakage. The wheat would spill on the ground in piles, especially in the train yard. Gene and the boys would shovel the grain into the gunny sacks, load the sacks in the trailer, and stop at the Dill company to sell the grain. Gene had a friend in the Dill Company who paid Gene cash for the wheat. The Dill Company man knew where the grain came from and looked the other way. It wasn't stealing. The wheat was going to rot on the ground anyway. It was like the Peery boys grabbing food from the boxcars during the Depression. The boys knew it wasn't legit, as Gene and the boys would hide behind a boxcar when a passenger train came by.

Wabasha started a youth baseball league in the summer. Mike and Terry joined the Westside Tigers. Gene Stroot and Bill Glomski were the volunteer coaches. There were volunteer umps as well. There were four teams in town based on neighborhood. Besides the Westside Tigers, there were the Dodgers, Braves, and White Sox. There was no Wabasha team named the Twins, because the Twins never came to

Minnesota until 1961, The team would practice a couple days a week and play two games a week. Since the Westside kids played baseball all summer in their yards, they were the team to beat. The saying for the team was "Westside is the best side." Everybody on the team would play at least one inning, so nobody felt left out. When you were eight and ten years old, you hardly could play with the sixteen-year-old boys. But Mike and Terry tried their best. The pitchers were important to the team. If you had a good pitcher, you could win a lot of games. The boys were not pitchers, so they alternated playing right field. Because the Westside was so isolated, the boys got to meet lots of boys their own age when they played other teams.

Westside Tigers baseball team.

Most would think the winter would dampen the Westside kids' adventures and playtime. That was far from the truth. Skating, sledding, and throwing snowballs at cars were the entertainment. Skating consumed most of the boys' free time. The city of Wabasha kept a skating rink in operation every day. Carl, a city employee, would work daily on the city rink. During the day he would spray water on the rink; it would freeze and make a slick and smooth surface for skating. The rink had lights for night skating and a warming house with a pot-belly wood stove. Carl also played music on a speaker system so the kids could dance while skating. Mike and Terry would walk to the rink and skate for hours. The greatest fun was playing crack the whip. A line of people would hold hands and skate in a circle faster and faster. Then the guy in the center of the rink would stop, anchor himself, and crack the whip. The outside skater would go flying, get airborne, and most of the time fly out of the rink. Mike and Terry would laugh at the boy flying out of the rink. The boys could play crack the whip all night. On weekends the rink would be packed with skaters.

Crack the whip at Wabasha skating rink

Mike and Terry complained to their dad about the crowds on weekends. Gene drove the Farmall Cub tractor to the slough below the house and plowed the snow for their own personal skating rink. On weekends, the boys would have skating parties. The day before the skating party, Mike and

Terry would chop or gather wood for the bonfire at night. All the Westside kids would come to the skating parties, roast marshmallows, and drink hot chocolate, and skate. They didn't have lights like the city skating rink, but the huge bonfire would provide enough light. They skated every weekend on the slough. Gene would plow the rink every Friday for the skating party.

If the boys got bored with skating, there would be sledding. There were lots of hills in Wabasha, and the best hill was from the boys' yard to the slough. In the fall Mike and Terry would cut the brush from the sledding hill. After the first snowfall, the boys would do a test run of the hill. If there wasn't enough snow, the boys would use the hose from the house and spray water down the hill. The hill would freeze, and Mike and Terry could sled. Icing the hill would make the boys almost go too fast down the hill. They crashed a lot with the iced hill. One Christmas Santa gave Mike and Terry a wooden toboggan. The boys couldn't steer the toboggan as well as the sleds, so the boys built a lip on both sides of the sledding hill with either snow or water from the hose that would freeze. The boys would water down the sledding hill, the water would freeze, and they would do a test run. When they iced the sledding hill, they could sled until spring. The boys got their inspiration from bobsled runs that they watched on TV. Finally it even looked like a bobsled hill. After two years of almost daily use and numerous crashes, the toboggan was totally destroyed. The boys used the destroyed toboggan for firewood when they were camping in the yard during the summer.

When there was a heavy, wet snow, the boys built giant snowmen. Mike and Terry used boards from the garage to

slide the middle and top pieces of the snowman into po-
sition. It took all their ingenuity and muscle to build the
snowman.

Stroot Kids building snowmen

If the boys were not building snowmen during a snowfall, they were pelting each other with snowballs. When the
boys would leave the Westside, they would pelt everyone,
especially girls. The boys would hide behind a building or a
tree, with their ammo ready, and pelt the girls with snowballs. The girls would scream and run away. When the boys
got bored with pelting girls, they would pelt cars. A few
drivers would get out of their car and chase the boys. Mike
and Terry knew the drivers could never catch them. Then
Leo Dick, on Bruegger's farm (where the Stroot family got
milk) built a ski hill. With old car engines and car wheels,
they built a tow rope. A warming hut on the bottom of
the hill with a wood stove provided the comfort the skiers
needed. The skiers used bear trap bindings (cable bindings),
which really did not work. The skiers could not easily turn.
The tow rope was another challenge. The skier had to gradu-
ally grip the rope, then follow the snow ruts to the top of the

hill. Mike and Terry skied on weekends at the Brueggers. They learned to ski in tough snow conditions with poor equipment. The boys liked skating and sledding much better than skiing.

The old farmhouse was as cold in the winter as it was hot in the summer. The two-story farmhouse had an oil burner in the kitchen and no heat in the second floor. There were grates in the second floor that let the heat rise from the first floor to the second floor. In January and February, there would be frost on the inside of the bedroom windows on the second floor. The kids could see their breath before they went to bed. During the winter, Fran and Gene would give the kids an extra blanket for warmth. The boys would leave their clothes for the next day near the bed and in the morning get dressed under the covers. After they got dressed under the covers, they would run downstairs to the oil burner to warm up. The kids walked to school regardless of the temperature.

When Terry reached his sixteenth birthday in January of 1965, he wanted to work and was expected to work. During the spring of that year, he dropped out of school for two weeks and went to work for the Milwaukee Railroad during the spring floods. The railroad hired lots of temporary workers to fill sandbags to protect their railroad line. Terry worked sixteen hours a day for fourteen straight days. But the principal of the school called Terry and his parents into his office for Terry's unexcused absence from school. It was a discussion with Gene and Fran and the principal; Terry kept quiet. Terry's parents talked about how Terry had to pay for his own college, and the principal retorted that Terry couldn't miss that much school. The conversation went round and round. They agreed Terry could skip school to work for a few days, but not two weeks straight.

That summer Terry and his buddies all got jobs with Lakeside Packing in Plainview. Five boys would carpool to Plainview and work twelve-hour shifts, seven days a week, at the minimum wage of $1.25 per hour. Lakeside Packing canned peas and corn from the local farmers. The only day the employees got off was a rain day. Terry worked for the railroad occasionally throughout the winter. After a snow-storm the railroad called Terry to shovel switches. The principal was fine with only one or two days of absence from school. Mike wanted to work, but he was not yet sixteen. So he sold worms for bait on the highway. He had a huge worm farm in the yard. He had an unlimited supply of worms. Mike would add the coffee grounds to the worm farm. The worms loved it.

CHAPTER 7

Characters

George Schuth was born in 1935 in Wabasha. He was given the nickname of Chicky from his grandma. As a kid, he loved electronics. He took apart radios and put them back together for fun. After high school, Chicky got a job with a local radio repair shop. When TVs started to appear, homes in Wabasha needed TV antennas on the roof to get reception. Chicky installed all the antennas. He could scamper up the steepest roofs with ease. Besides fixing TVs and radios and installing antennas, he was a volunteer fireman. He applied for and was turned down by the fire department as a firetruck driver. Chicky really wanted to drive the firetruck, with its lights and siren. After a few beers at the Westside Tavern, he walked to the fire station, used his key, and took the fire truck for a spin. He noisily blew the siren and lit up all the lights. Someone called the sheriff and reported Chicky.

Sheriff Ed Lager checked it out. It was not hard for Sheriff Lager to find Chicky and the wayward firetruck. Sheriff Lager called the fire chief, Gene Stroot. Gene and Ed pulled Chicky over and talked with him. They headed back to the fire station, with Chicky in Sheriff Lager's patrol car and Gene driving the firetruck. Gene turned off the sirens and lights. Ed and Gene talked about what to do about Chicky. They decided to take the fire station key away from Chicky. He was a good fireman, and there was no need to punish him. Chicky learned his lesson. No reports were written by Sheriff Lager and the fire chief. The case was closed. After twenty years of great service, Chicky retired from the Wabasha Fire Department. They had a party for Chicky, and most of the town showed up.

Another character was Scumpy.

Lloyd Schomp was born in 1896 across the river in Alma, Wisconsin. He served in World War I, and after the war he moved to Wabasha. He built an eight-by-twenty-four-foot shack on the bank of the Mississippi River under the bridge in downtown Wabasha. He had no elec-

Scumpys Shack on river

tricity, no plumbing, and a coal stove. He rounded up coal from the spillage from the railroad cars on the tracks. In the summer he bathed in the river; in the winter he washed up in a bucket. He was an expert fishing guide. Scumpy's favorite clients were the doctors from the Mayo Clinic. Local woman would bring him food, especially during the holidays. In real cold weather, he would sleep in the basement of Dan Foley's law office. In return Scumpy would stoke Dan Foley's coal furnace. Everybody looked after Scumpy. Even the chief of police, Curt Goetz, would check on him every morning. Wabasha even celebrated Scumpy Days at the American Legion.

Scumpy was a true river rat. He may not have lived in the best house in town, but his real home and love was the Mississippi River. From his front door, he had a million-dollar view of the river. Finally, Scumpy's shack burned down in 1967. He was seventy years old, and he didn't have the energy to start over. He retired to a nursing home and died in 1969 at the age of seventy-two. He lived his life his way. The river was his playground and backyard. Most people considered him a bum, but he was rich in so many ways.

As Scumpy's shack burned down, he was replaced by another river rat. That river rat was Slippery Bach, born in Milwaukee in 1928. Slippery had served in the Army during World War II. After his discharge from the army, Slippery went home to Milwaukee to work for one of the many meat packing companies. The Milwaukee meat packing industry started out small, with neighborhood butcher shops. As Milwaukee grew, some butcher shops grew into large operations. In 1869, the Milwaukee Railroad constructed stockyards along one of the rail yards, patterned after the Chicago Union stockyards, which had opened four years earlier. It was a huge success. By 1880, meat packing was Milwaukee's leading industry. Prior to refrigeration, Lake Michigan had unlimited ice for the meat packing industry. Cudahy Brothers and Armour had substantial operations in Milwaukee. World Wars I and II provided military contracts that expanded the Milwaukee meat packing industry further. Milwaukee was noted for making sausages primarily because the German immigrants brought their sausage-making skills with them.

After World War II, the Milwaukee meat packing industry started a slow decline. On Slippery's first week of work, he met Al Wilson, who was born near Wabasha. Al Wilson didn't like the meat packing industry or Milwaukee. He wanted to move back to Wabasha, but Al married a girl from Wisconsin Rapids, and she didn't want to leave Wisconsin. During lunch, Al would tell Slippery about fishing on the Mississippi River. That got Slippery's attention, because he had loved fishing as a kid and hated his job cutting up beef on an assembly line. One night Al asked Slippery to go for a beer after work at the local tavern. On the way to the tavern, Al told Slippery that his wife was working that night in the tavern. Al introduced Slippery to his wife Gladys. They all exchanged pleasantries and got to the subject at hand, fishing. That night Al and Slippery hatched a plan for a fishing trip to Wabasha. Al would break it to Gladys the next morning. Gladys was hesitant, because she wanted to visit her friends in Wisconsin Rapids.

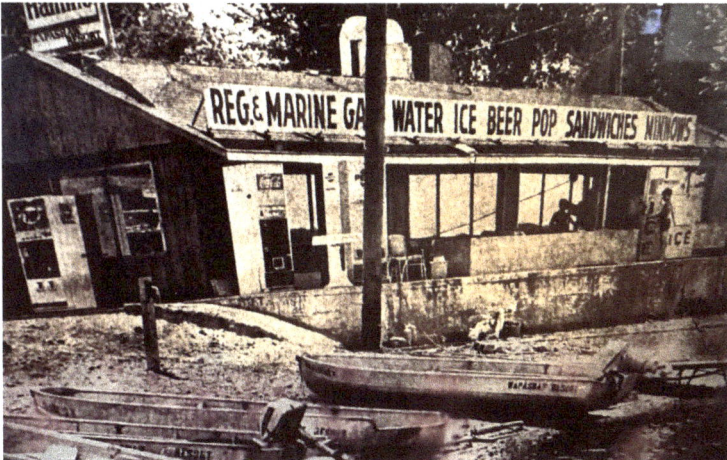

Wapashaw Resort(Slipperies)

They picked a week when they all had vacation and drove to Wabasha. They stayed at the Wapashaw Resort in two tiny cabins. Wapashaw Resort had everything they needed: cabins, bait, boats, and beer. They fished all day and drank beer all night. Gladys was a natural at fishing. She could clean the fish like an old pro. One night Ray Kirsch, the owner of the resort, was tending bar, and he was complaining the resort was too much work for one man and he might sell the resort. Al and Slippery perked up at the mention of the resort for sale. On the way home to Milwaukee, the trio talked nonstop about buying the resort. Al wanted to move back home to Wabasha, Slippery hated his job, and Gladys was still glowing from catching so many fish. Al would cook, Gladys could waitress, and Slippery could be the fish guide and fill in as a cook.

Gladys was the reluctant one. Her parents still lived in Wisconsin Rapids, and she would miss them as they were getting older. The first week at work at the meat packing plant was brutal for Al and Slippery after spending a glorious week fishing. After work Al and Slippery met Gladys at the tavern and talked about buying the resort. Gladys was all in for buying the resort. She had just spent a night in Wisconsin Rapids with her parents. Gladys's parents were all for Gladys buying the resort. Gladys didn't have to worry about them; they would be fine. The three of them decided to buy the resort. Slippery would call Ray Kirsch. He wasn't nicknamed "Slippery" for nothing. He well deserved his nickname. He was the perfect one of the three to negotiate the price and the sale of the resort. Slippery called Ray the next day and struck a deal. After they pooled all their money for the purchase of the Wapashaw Resort, they still came up short. Luckily Gladys's parents lent them the balance of the money to buy the resort.

The resort would change hands in April of 1967. All three of them were so excited. The trio planned daily for their new adventure. At the end of March, they all quit their jobs, packed their clothes, and drove to Wabasha. Wapashaw Resort was a success from the beginning. The trio worked hard, and the burgers were good. They settled into a routine. Al would cook, Gladys would wait tables, and Slippery would manage the bait shop and take people on fishing trips. If Slippery didn't have customers to take fishing, he would fill in cooking. He developed a juicy burger called the Slippery burger. Slippery's reputation as a fishing guide soon spread. A columnist from the *Star Tribune* was in town for a weekend, and he hired Slippery as a fishing guide. Slippery took him to his favorite fishing hole. Slippery bet the columnist "One cast, five pound northern." The columnist agreed to the bet. One cast later, Slippery reeled in a five-pound, two-ounce northern. Slippery's reputation as a fishing guide was cemented from that day forward.

Wapashaw Resort became known locally as Slippery's. The trio had good run for twelve years. They had polka music on weekends with Eddie Z. The weekends were packed. Then the tavern/bait shop burned down in 1979. The trio rebuilt the tavern, but it was never the same with the new and updated building. The new Slippery's Tavern didn't have the ambience and character like the old Slippery's. After the new tavern had been operating for a few years, the trio decided to sell it to a few local businessmen. Slippery worked at a different tavern in town. Slippery, Gladys, and Al were missing the old place. Al moved to Theilman, where he was born. He died in 1994 at the age of seventy-nine. Gladys divorced Al and, within a few weeks, married Slippery. Gladys died in 1989 at seventy-two years old. Slippery died in 1992 at sixty-three. Gladys and Slippery are buried together in Wabasha. Their true love was Wabasha, fishing, and each other, in that order.

Old timers around town will still tell stories of the old Slippery's Tavern. Like Slippery himself, don't believe the tales. They might be true or just fish tales. Slippery's reputation was etched in stone when the movie *Grumpy Old Men* debuted in 1993. He died a year before the movie came out. He didn't need to see the movie; he lived it.

The last character was Jakie Mathias. Jacob was born in Wabasha in 1900. As a kid, he loved riverboats cruising on the Mississippi River. If his parents noticed Jacob was missing, they could always find him on the riverbank near the Peters Wabasha Boat Works. The Peters Boat Works overhauled small riverboats and built a total of five new riverboats. They also built the pontoon bridge that the Milwaukee Railroad used to cross the river from Reads Landing to Wisconsin. Jakie hung out at the Peters Boat Works so much he was offered job at sixteen. He dropped out of high school and took his dream job of building riverboats.

Riverboats saw their demise as the railroads completed their tracks everywhere in America. The last river boat that Peters Boat Yard built was the *Aquila* in 1928. The demise of the riverboats along with the Great Depression was too much for Peters Boat Works. It shut down in December 1935. Jakie was out of job. He didn't have much or need much. He was single and lived in a shack on an alley downtown. After his last day of work, Jakie walked to the Westside

Tavern to drown his sorrows. He met the Westside railroad men who were also drowning their sorrows. Jakie was asking the railroad men about jobs on the railroad. They all laughed. The Milwaukee Railroad was laying off, not hiring. They pointed to Ben Peery at the end of the bar. They told Jakie to ask him about a job. Ben worked for the Post Office sorting mail on passenger trains.

Jakie introduced himself to Ben Peery and bought him a beer. Jakie asked how he could get a job with the Post Office. Ben laughed. Ben bought Jakie a beer. They talked about the Westside, the depression, and beer for hours. It started snowing now, and Ben had to go home to supper. He only had a block to walk and Jakie had a long walk ahead of him. The bartender heard that Jakie was going to walk home during a snowstorm. The bartender called Lawrence Stroot who was the cop in town. Lawrence had a cop car and gave Jakie a ride home. The next day, Jakie had a decision to make. There were no jobs to be found anywhere. He had only one skill and that was building riverboats.

He started building model riverboats from scrap cardboard and popsicle sticks. He scrounged up a few tools. The tools included paper punches and knives. He set up a workbench in his shack. He knew most of the riverboat captains plying the river still. This included the captain of the *Avalon* and Captain Earnie Wagner of the *Delta Queen*. Jakie gave some of his model boats away to people that helped him and cared for him. The undertaker hired him to answer phones while he working funerals. He got a model riverboat. The women of town brought him food; they got a model boat. The Westside Tavern and Grocery Store got a model boat, letting him drink beer for free and giving him a few groceries. The sheriff Ed Lager, got two boats for giving Jakie a ride home in inclement weather or when he had too much to drink. Ed Lager was the sheriff when he stopped Chicky Schuth from driving the firetruck drunk. Jakie died in 1976. Jakie built eighty model riverboats over his lifetime. They are in museums, libraries and homes. His legacy is riverboats from scrap cardboard and popsicle sticks he scavenged. The town took care of Jakie and he repaid the town with model riverboats.

CHAPTER 8

Conclusion

What did Westside of Wabasha have that they accepted all sorts of characters? Let us be clear—not everyone was accepting of the characters. There were the usual bullies who liked to pick on the weaklings. The town not only accepted the characters, but embraced them, cared for them, and celebrated them. The town had Scumpy Days, where they celebrated a bum who lived in a shack by the river. Here are a few thoughts.

POVERTY. The people of Wabasha, especially the Westside, were all in the same boat—the boat was named *Dirt Poor*. No one could gloat or hold their neighbors in contempt.

IMMIGRANTS. The Germans and Swedes were hardworking people who struggled mightily to get to Wabasha. Gustava was one, who traveled alone at fifty-eight to Minnesota. She went from a stagecoach to a ship to a train across England to a ship to New York to a train to Chicago, walking to different depots, and finally to a train to Minneiska. Gustava never saw her children or her native Sweden again. All because her brother asked her to come to America and raise his daughters. Theodore and Adelaide Roemer, who, at fifty-two and fifty, made the arduous journey to Wabasha with four kids. They were all hardy people who wanted a better life for themselves and their children in America. The immigrants, so to speak, were in the same boat.

NATURAL BEAUTY. Slippery left Milwaukee because he loved the river and fishing. He followed his passion, as did his predecessor, Scumpy.

SMALL RURAL TOWN. Wabasha, especially the Westside, was a poor, tight-knit community where people cared for their neighbors. The gruff chief of police went out of his way to check on Scumpy every morning. When Ben Peery started flying model airplanes in his new neighborhood in Minneapolis, he was ridiculed. He soon realized his new town didn't accept characters like Wabasha did. Dan Foley let Scumpy stay in his law office basement on a cold day. Caroline Peery gave a few coins to the Westside neighbors or invited the hobos to dine with her family. Nelson Peery came back to Wabasha in 2009 and was quoted as saying, "I was fortunate to have grown to maturity in Wabasha, where I met with much more curiosity and acceptance than antagonism. My early life experiences here in Wabasha gave me the notion that everyone was as good as me. That meant to this day, I cannot discriminate or feel badly toward anyone simply because of the color of their skin."

NO SCREENS. The whistle blew at noon and 6:00 p.m., when the kids would drop what they were doing and run home for food. Adventure and play outside was a daily part of life. Nobody had TVs or cell phones. The kids had to create their own games and entertainment. If you were lucky, your grandma would have a TV. Every Saturday kids would bike to their grandma's and watch TV and listen to grandma's stories.

Epilogue

The stories of Grandma Inez (Roemer) Stroot, who witnessed Northwest mail planes flying over her Beacon Farm, resonated with Terry. Even though he worked hard every summer, he could not afford to pay for private flying lessons and pay for college at the same time. December 1, 1969, was the first draft lottery since 1942. The lottery was televised, and everyone of draft age was glued to the TV. Terry got a lottery number of 318. He never had to go into the military. But he still wanted to learn to fly. As with all poor boys, the military was the only option. He went to the Navy and Air Force recruiter and filled out an application for pilot training. The Air Force accepted him in March of 1971. He was excited to get a pilot training slot, except for the unpopular Vietnam war. Most of Terry's friends were against him going into the Air Force during the war. He was going into the

Northwest 747-400 which Terry flew as Captain for 8 Years till retirement.

Air Force regardless of his friends' opinions. But he needed one more opinion. That opinion that mattered most was his dad's. Gene was a Marine in World War II and grew up in the Depression on the Westside.

Gene said, "The Air Force is going to make you officer and teach you to fly? What is the problem?" Gene said, "Go for it."

Terry signed the Air Force papers the next day. After six years in the Air Force, he got hired by Northwest Airlines. Several times he flew down the river as a pilot for Northwest Airlines, looking for the Beacon Farm, where his grandma was born. He never saw the Beacon Farm from the air. The beacon had been decommissioned in 1945. Inez (Roemer) Stroot died in 1969. She never saw her grandson in his pilot's uniform. But she had planted the seed of flying with her stories about mail planes flying over Beacon Farm and her stories about her heroes, Charles Lindbergh, Amelia Earhart, Bessie Coleman, and Beryl Markham.

Milton Keynes UK
Ingram Content Group UK Ltd.
UKHW020732071024
449371UK00011B/843